# BENEATH THE SURFACE

# BENEATH THE SURFACE

FRANK SLATER

ISBN: 979-8-218-43812-8 (paperback)
ISBN: 979-8-218-47067-8 (hardcover)

*For my wife Faye*

# PROLOGUE

Martha's eyes cracked open to a blurry darkness, and she wondered why she couldn't see clearly. This thought was pushed aside as she felt the intense throbbing in her head. She closed her eyes and became aware of a familiar sound and struggled to remember—and then it came. It was the comforting sound of heavy rain beating on the tin roof of her childhood home. She hoped she would wake up in her old bed. Feeling wind and rain against her left cheek, she rubbed her eyes only to find that her hands were wet, salty. The sense she was in trouble overcame her, but she couldn't identify why.

She felt like she was enveloped in a thick fog. Her feet felt wet. *But why?* She tried to think but couldn't focus. *Am I standing in water? No, I'm sitting.* This bewildered her, and for a moment, she became upset. She liked being in control, but right now, she didn't know why she was sitting in the dark, with a soggy glow of lights in front of her and warm water now slapping at her knees.

Moments later, she felt like she'd wet her pants. *My God, what's happening?* she wondered. *Where am I?* As she moaned, her hands found a steering wheel. *I'm in the car. In a river? How? Why?* She could feel the seat belt pressing against her. *I must unbuckle it,* she decided. She turned to find the seat belt, but the water was now up to her breasts. She couldn't find the latch. It was all happening so fast. She saw someone sitting in the front seat staring at her, not moving. But she couldn't tell who it was. *Why aren't they helping me?* It was so dark, and she felt so tired. Laying her head back against the head rest, she closed her eyes. The water now reached her shoulders—then her chin. *I'm so scared.* In slow motion, her arms flung wildly under the water as she struggled in her seat. She leaned her head back again, but the water would not stop. Although she tried to scream, only a gurgling sound escaped. *The water's so salty.* Then darkness closed in.

Only the trail of bubbles rising to the surface of the river marked where Martha Willis, professor emerita of English literature, sat.

# CHAPTER 1



*Seven Hours Earlier*

Shafts of late morning sunlight streamed through the tall hardwoods, throwing splashes of light on the shaded front lawn. Henry stood on his front porch looking out, hands in his pockets, standing rigid, his breathing short and shallow. The cool early summer breeze that rustled the leaves did little to comfort him. Shaking his head, he wished he didn't have to go to the party in Charleston, but Martha had insisted, and he knew, rightfully so.

The joint retirement ceremony for him and Martha, after thirty years at Southern College in Asheville, had been an emotional farewell for them both. Henry's energy and socializing capacity had faded after less than an hour at the cocktail reception afterward. Martha told him later she was pleased he lasted that long.

Now, she called to him that it was time to leave, pulling him from his trance. Henry walked to their car, helped load the suitcases, and with Martha behind the wheel, they headed for Charleston. Henry steeled himself for the upcoming social event and slumped in his seat.

Martha glanced over at him.

"Cheer up, Henry. After all these years, we'll soon be on our way to England again. It's been twenty years since we've visited Shakespeare's country."

Henry sat up at the thought and managed to smile.

"I know, and it'll be like a new beginning for us. I just wish we were on our way now." His smile faded. "I'm not so sure about this gathering at Charleston College. I know it's our sister college, but I don't know many people down there like you do."

"You'll be just fine. Lots of folks from Asheville are coming, and of course, Emily will be there. It might be an opportunity to begin reconnecting with your daughter. She's already in grad school so you have some catching up to do. It'll be fine. I know it will."

Henry sighed and stared out the window.

"You know, we're returning to where it all began for us so many years ago," said Martha, reminiscing. "Meeting by chance at the college our senior year, for the English conference that week. You were in town from UNC and after the last presentation, we went out to that little pub down the street for a beer and a burger. That was our beginning."

Henry grinned at the thought.

"Yes, it was," he murmured.

He smiled, remembering that at the time he didn't realize it was the start of a new life for him. For a moment he thought back on it, then he frowned.

"You don't think Jack Townsend will be there tonight, do you? I still haven't forgotten what he did with you when we were dating."

"Nor have I," said Martha. "He took me out that one night and you got in a fight with him a day later." She looked over and smiled. "I believe you came out on the short end of that, but I was proud of you for standing up to him."

Henry felt his chest tighten at the memory of that confrontation.

"But Jack kept after you for years," he said, "sending Christmas cards, birthday cards, and on and on it went."

"It all faded away, Henry." She reached over and playfully patted him on the arm.

But it never faded away for Henry. Henry closed his eyes. His fight with Jack triggered dark memories of a life-changing incident back in high school. The guilt over his actions made him withdraw into a shell that had ruled his temperament most of his adult life. They drove on in silence, listening to classical music on NPR as the Blue Ridge Mountains faded onto the piedmont and midlands of South Carolina and then to the low country and the moss-draped live oaks and azaleas of Charleston.

They arrived around five o'clock, and Emily was there to greet them. The folks inside gave them a round of applause along with some cheers and whistles. The open bar was doing a brisk business that encouraged the festive atmosphere.

Martha moved through the well-wishers, talking briefly to each as Henry followed behind, nodding and smiling. They were standing on one side of the room talking to a colleague when they noticed the din of the small talk began to taper off. Looking around, they saw a few people glancing surreptitiously over at them and whispering. A minute later Emily, looking alarmed, made her way over to Martha and Henry and whispered that a rumor was circulating that Henry recently had a one-night affair with a girl in his graduate class. Martha stared ahead, her teeth clenched. She turned to Henry, opened her mouth as if to speak, then closed it, staring at him. The blood drained from Henry's face. He blinked, eyes wide. His mouth opened, but no words came out. Martha looked as if this told her all she needed to know and what she needed to do.

She whispered to him, "We're leaving the party right now. First, I have to explain to certain people that you are feeling sick and we're very sorry, but we need to leave. And thank them for honoring us. Stay here."

He managed to place their drinks on a nearby table without spilling them. His heart throbbing and short of breath, his mind racing, he was fearful of what Martha would do and what he would say. He stood facing a bookcase, his shoulders slumped, in shock, his mind blank.

She returned and tapped on his shoulder. As he turned, he saw the scowl on her face that said it all—a look of both anger and embarrassment.

Without a word, she took his hand and began leading him toward the door. She apologized to people along the way, saying Henry was not feeling well and thanking them for the party. In the entry way, Martha stood eye to eye with Henry, without blinking and, just above a whisper, said, "Follow me." She turned and strode out the front door.

# CHAPTER 2

Any thought of a pardon for his one-night stand with the leggy Italian grad student half his age dwindled as Henry Willis struggled to stay behind Martha, who marched straight backed down the sidewalk in the steaming heat of early evening, cutting a swath through the crowd of tourists filling the streets of Charleston. Low black clouds roiled over the rooftops of the historic buildings. The wind began to gust. Henry feared the weather might be a precursor of what he was about to face.

Martha came to Chez Toulouse, opened the front door, waved off Francois, the maître d', and strode by him.

"Your favorite table by the window is ready for you, Mrs. Willis," he said to her back.

Martha took a seat facing the door. She was dressed in a buttoned-up white silk blouse and a dark blue jacket, her glasses hanging from a thin chain around her neck.

Seconds later, Henry stepped inside, glanced over at Martha, sitting with her chin up just a notch, and stopped. Sweating and out of breath, his rimless spectacles fogged, his mouth dry and ears ringing, he shook his head and debated whether he had the courage to continue on toward her. He wondered if he had squandered their marriage of thirty years. He had never seen her look so embarrassed and furious. Henry knew well that Martha was most upset because this would be viewed as a significant blemish on their spotless careers, a juicy scandal to be remembered by.

Henry walked to the table, hung his frayed tweed jacket on the back of the chair, and straightened his tie, hoping to deflect a comment from his wife. He fell into his seat across from her, avoiding her stare as he tried to slow his heartbeat. The smell of rich food distracted him for a moment as he lined up the polished silverware nervously.

The flickering candle and mahogany wainscoting below the oil paintings of the French countryside—which usually comforted Henry—offered little respite. The sudden splattering of large raindrops, driven by the wind against their window, did not distract them. Aware that she was waiting for his explanation, his usually quick mind was not ready for this type of expository challenge, and he tried cleaning his glasses—but it only delayed the inevitable.

Martha had not spoken since he arrived, so he began to stumble though his explanation of how, a few weeks before, he had been seduced by this young woman into his first transgression in their marriage. Before he ventured far into his confession and plea for understanding, their waiter appeared with menus and their customary bottle of cabernet, a smile on his face. Henry hoped for a temporary reprieve by selecting an appetizer. But under Martha's stare, the waiter—now at attention—poured two glasses, set the bottle on the table, and retreated without a word. Sweating profusely, Henry wiped his brow with his napkin.

"What's her name?" she asked in an even tone, staring at him unblinking.

Henry started in, distinctly aware that he was mumbling.

"Sophia Bandini, a transfer grad student from New York. Her father was Italian." He immediately wished he had not lengthened his answer with unnecessary details.

Although Martha looked at him, he could not meet her eyes. He took a deep breath, ready to push on. As he looked up, he saw Martha holding up her hand, motioning him to stop. His eyes wide, he held his breath, not moving.

"Henry, I don't need to hear anymore."

He was confused, his eyes blinking. He didn't know what to say, what she meant. He didn't move.

"I'd like the coq au vin tonight," she announced, staring at him with blank eyes.

Henry saw her glance over his shoulder at something, first with a look of shock and then of alarm.

Henry looked behind him and saw the man standing by the door looking at them. He gasped as he turned back to Martha.

"Is that…?" he whispered. He turned and took another quick look, watching as the man started toward their table. "What's he doing here?" he muttered under his breath.

"I'll take care of this," she said, setting her wine down and sitting up, her hands folded on the table.

The man stopped in front of them, wiping the raindrops from his forehead with his handkerchief. His light blue sport coat was splattered with rain. He looked at Martha and said, "Excuse me, but I believe you're Martha Willis."

Martha nodded. "Hello, Jack," she said.

He shook his head, as if in disbelief. "You're as beautiful as ever."

"And you remember my husband, Henry, of course," said Martha, glancing toward Henry.

Smiling, Jack nodded at Henry, who stared back without a response.

Henry worked hard at controlling his anger at this man standing over him. In college, when Henry was dating Martha, Jack had succeeded in getting a date with her on a night Henry was studying for an exam. Later, Martha told Henry that Jack had pressed her to have sex with him, but she had managed to deflect him. When Henry had confronted him over this, Jack had denied it and belted him. Henry had not fought back, not with the memories of his ugly high school incident still stamped in his head. Now, here Jack stood, the tall, handsome jet pilot, dressed in his expensive clothes and his full head of hair, and flirting with his wife. Henry still felt outgunned by Jack.

For a moment no one spoke.

Martha broke the silence.

"Why don't you join us, just for a moment?" she said, cordially.

Surprised at Martha's invitation, Henry looked startled. He recalled all the years Jack harassed Martha with his letters, boasting of his latest exploits, trying to get her attention. Jesus, they couldn't get him to stop.

Now, here he is, thought Henry, pushing himself on Martha again.

Martha took the middle road.

"Jack, you can stay for five minutes. We'll all be civil and then you'll leave. Agreed?"

A wide grin came over his face.

"Agreed," he said, pulling over a chair and sitting down at the end of their table.

The waiter approached. Before Henry could wave him off, the waiter asked Jack if he would like something to drink.

"A bourbon on the rocks. Your best," he said, pulling out his wallet and dropping a fifty-dollar bill on the table. "This should take care of my drink, along with another round for my friends here."

"Well, it's so great to see you again," said Jack, looking at Martha. "My, it's hard to believe I met you my first year in college, just down the street."

The waiter returned with Jack's drink, who raised his glass as if to make a toast.

Martha cut him off. "Are they still letting you fly airplanes, Jack?" she asked.

"Sure are, and I still love it. Flying for a commuter airline out of Charleston now, covering the Carolinas." He sipped on his drink. "Damn, what a nice surprise to find you all here," he said.

Well into his second glass of wine, Henry wondered, is Martha punishing me by her polite behavior to Jack? Henry was not an instigator. To temper Martha's charitable words to Jack, he slipped into his "professor speak," which Henry knew irritated him.

"Well, Jack, did you come to apprise us of your current marital circumstances?"

Jack looked at Henry and cocked his head.

"I see you're still trying to confuse us regular folks with your vocabulary." He smiled. "But I think I follow your question. My wife died recently in a swimming accident, and our only son lives out west."

A silence fell over the table.

Jack picked it up again. "So, I'm back in the mix and I'm still waiting on that special woman," he said, glancing at Martha for a second.

This did not go unnoticed by Henry. "Jack," he said, "you must excuse us so we can order our dinner."

Before Jack could answer, Martha said, "Let him finish his drink, Henry. That should be the end."

Henry didn't like to be overruled in front of this man, but given tonight's circumstances, he was on good behavior with Martha. Maybe she's right. After this, we're done with him.

Smiling at Martha, Jack nodded before looking at Henry.

"You know, I'd sure like to find a woman like your Martha." He turned back to her. "But I doubt there's another lady like her around."

Henry had had enough.

"Jack, it's time for you to leave. I'd prefer not to have to call the maître d' over to escort you out of here." He noticed a stare from Martha and wondered, Does she enjoy this cheap flattery from this guy?

Of all things, with such bad timing, Henry, who had been holding off making a trip to the men's room, squirmed in his seat as his bladder signaled it was time—now. He was forced to excuse himself and leave, cursing how at his age one of the basic functions in life could become so embarrassing.

Jack looked back at Henry until he disappeared around the corner. Looking again at Martha, he put his hand on top of hers. She looked at him and smiled. Staring at him a moment, she said, "Jack, this fairytale of yours is over."

She pulled her hand away, her gaze now level and cool. "And if you ever try to contact me again, I will go to the police. Do you understand?"

"But I thought you said we were going to take off and drive…" he began just as Henry walked up.

Henry noticed the look on Martha's face as she stared at Jack.

"Martha, are you all right?" he asked, taking his seat. Henry hoped that whatever it was, it was over, and he would not have to confront Jack.

"No, Henry," said Martha. "There'll be no more problems here. Jack is leaving us. Forever. Isn't that correct, Jack?"

Jack suddenly stood, knocking his chair over backward, banging hard into the table and toppling the two wine glasses, sending red wine spewing across the white tablecloth. He put his hands on the table and leaned over and stared at Martha.

Just above a whisper, he said, "You don't give me orders!"

With deliberation, he picked up his cocktail glass, took a long drink and then slammed it down, sending some ice cubes flying. He looked at Henry.

"There's fifty dollars on the table. That should take care of my drink and the mess."

Jack turned back to Martha. Before he could speak, in an even tone, she said, "Time for you to leave, Jack. Save your antics for a bar."

Glaring at her, he slammed his hands down on the table. The glasses jumped again. He started for the door, bumped into Francois, knocked him aside, and strode out, leaving the door wide open, the wind-driven rain blowing in.

Henry and Martha looked at each other, speechless. Henry stared back at the open door in disbelief. He turned back as Francois approached the table, asking if they were all right and should he call the police. The restaurant chatter had come to a halt.

"No need for that," said Martha. "We had a disagreement and he got upset. He recently lost his wife and is more unnerved by that than I think he realizes. We're fine and apologize for the uproar we created. I think we'll just sit here a moment and gather our thoughts."

Almost hyperventilating, Henry looked at Martha and cried, "My God, he's crazy!" He took a deep breath, calming himself down. "What happened while I was gone? Before I left, everything was all hearts and flowers from him. And suddenly, he's off the rails, knocking over glasses and storming out."

"Jack tried to hold my hand when you were gone, and I told him to go away. Apparently, he doesn't like to be ordered about. He'll cool off in the rain."

Henry shook his head.

"He scares me…how he acts. What he might do." He exhaled deeply. "He tried to hold your hand? Jesus."

She reached across the table and took his hand. "It's over, Henry. He's gone."

A team of waiters appeared, cleared the table before setting a new tablecloth and dinner settings. Two fresh glasses of wine were set along with an appetizer of escargots and bread.

They picked at the appetizer in silence. After a minute, Martha took a sip of her wine and stared at Henry over the rim of her glass.

"I didn't think you had it in you—" she said, hesitating, "—to have an affair."

Caught by surprise, Henry didn't know how to respond. She didn't think I was man enough to have a one-night affair or that I was brave enough to cheat on her? He went with, "I'm sorry that I did what I did."

"I'd like to put your recent indiscretion behind us," she said. "Who knows, maybe it relighted some fires in you?"

Henry just stared at her, his mouth half open.

A smile crossed her face. "Henry, I believe you're blushing."

Still somewhat unsure, he hesitated before raising his glass. "Here's to us," he said.

"Yes, here's to us," she said. "In a month, we'll be on our way to England, driving in a red convertible, the wind in our hair. The beginning of a new chapter in our lives."

His head spinning from the various turn of events over the last few hours, Henry finally felt it had all, somehow, come to a wonderful conclusion. He finally relaxed, marveling again at how beautiful his wife looked; her auburn hair and deep green eyes in the candlelight. He reflexively ran his hand through his unruly, gray-streaked hair and over his beard. He knew he was a lucky man. Martha could have had any man she wanted, and she chose him.

"How about room service at the hotel?" asked Henry. "I'll buy."

"You've got a date. I'll go get the car out of the parking garage." She looked out at the heavy rain. "I hope they still keep umbrellas here for their customers."

"Wait, let me pay up and I'll go with you," said Henry. "And let me drive in this weather."

"There's no need for that. The car is less than a block away. I'll meet you here, then you can direct us to the hotel. By the time you get the check and pay, I'll be waiting for you out front."

"Okay, okay. You win." Signaling for the check, he walked her to the front, picked up two umbrellas, and opened the door.

Beneath the awning, they stepped out into early darkness as gusts of wind buffeted them. "Mon Dieu," he exclaimed.

"See you in a few minutes," she said, opening her umbrella in the wind and starting down the sidewalk toward the side street less than a hundred feet away.

Henry stood and watched as she struggled to cross the street in the storm.

"Wait, Martha," he called out. "I'm coming!" But his words were lost in the wind. He was about to step out after her but lost sight of her as she turned the corner. *She'll be fine without my tagging along*, he thought. *She always is.*

Little did he realize this one hesitation would change everything.

# CHAPTER 3

Back in the restaurant, he returned to their table and saw there was no leather folder with the check. He spotted Francois in a far corner of the room, who signaled him to wait. Henry sat and sipped his wine, replaying the scene with Jack Townsend in his mind. Henry wished he had been the one to send him packing instead of Martha. He needed to have the last word with him. Finishing his wine and tired of waiting, he stood to leave when Francois appeared and told him there would be no charge for the evening. Henry pulled out three twenties, pressed them into his hand, thanked him, and hurried outside. He was suddenly concerned that Martha had been waiting for some time, worried that her forgiving mood might have disappeared.

He found only the wind, rain, and near darkness. Surprised, he glanced at his watch and saw it had been at least ten or fifteen minutes since she'd left. He looked up and down the street into darkness and felt the first hint that something might be wrong. Under the restaurant awning, he turned his back to the wind and called her cell phone. It did not connect. Nothing. Passing cars with their lights on threw up sheets of water as the street began to flood.

An elderly couple came out of the restaurant without an umbrella. Henry gave them his. He tried to think of a reason why Martha had not returned and the reason for the sudden loss of cell phone service. But he couldn't think coherently. All he knew for sure was that he should have gone to the car with her in this storm. A section of lights in the block across the street flickered and went dark, followed by more down the street. He looked around. Feeling lost and frantic, he became lightheaded as seeds of panic began to appear.

Henry realized he had to move, to do something other than stand under the awning waiting. But the fear of what might lie ahead nearly paralyzed him. Almost entranced, he walked out into the storm, beginning his trek to the parking garage. Great curtains of rain pounded the streets and ran toward storm drains that were already backed up, unable to digest the torrent of water being forced on them.

In half a block and soaked to the skin, Henry paused to catch his breath. Crossing the street in the wind and rushing water that had now begun to cover the sidewalks became a test of balance and fortitude. Marching on, he noticed that the lights were out on both sides of the deserted street. It could be three in the morning, he thought.

Out of breath when he reached the parking garage, Henry managed to stumble through the entrance. Huddling just inside, out of the wind and rain, he bent over to gasp for air. He sat down on the concrete walkway. His sedentary lifestyle had not prepared him for even this short journey. Darkness surrounded him. How could it be there are no lights? Although the temperature was still in the eighties, a chill passed over him.

He tried her cell phone again, but nothing. He thought to turn on his cell phone flashlight, but it seemed to take forever to figure out how to do it. Remembering they were parked on the third level, he forced himself up and began a march up the ramp. He prayed that he would find her in the car waiting out the storm, her cell phone wet and not working, waiting for him to come.

He walked and stumbled as fast as his tired body would carry him up the ramp toward the third level, checking for their car along the way. Not remembering exactly where they parked on the third deck, he glanced back and forth in the darkness at the few remaining parked cars. He searched for the familiar sight of their dark blue Buick with North Carolina plates and the Southern College parking sticker. Sweating profusely, Henry leaned against one of the cars and tried to slow his heart rate. For a moment, he thought he might faint. The wind howled as the rain swept through the wall openings and now reached the center of the garage. Moments later, the emergency lights came on, casting an eerie glow over the wet concrete and the few remaining cars.

As he neared the beginning of the fourth level, Henry came to the frightening realization that their car may not be in the garage. To be sure, he stumbled to the fourth level but saw only one vehicle, a black Hummer. Just the sight of it triggered a reflex in him: I hate those monsters. Since entering the garage, he had not seen anybody, or any car coming or going. There was no one to ask for help.

Back down to the third level, he searched again. Spinning around, he knew they had parked on the third. They had both said it out loud so they would remember. Dazed, he collapsed and sat on the concrete deck exhausted, with a mounting fear that something terrible had happened. Martha was not one to take chances or get herself in trouble. She had been out in this type of weather before, but not after a dinner and a confrontation with Jack Townsend, extra wine, and so little food. Why hasn't she called? It's been an hour since she left. As his eyes swelled with tears, his head fell to his chest, afraid to confront the possibility that his wife may be in serious trouble. He sat alone, lost in the deafening roar of the wind and rain that poured incessantly through the garage.

After some minutes, Henry pulled himself up, leaned against the back end of a small car and called their daughter, Emily—now a grad student at the college—and hoped she would pick up. Although she was expected to sit with them at the retirement banquet, after the rumors of his affair swept the room and reached her, he was sure Emily understood why Martha had yanked him out of there.

When she answered, he sagged in relief. He took a deep breath to steady himself. In a trembling voice, barely above a whisper, he said, "I've lost Mom."

"Is that you, Dad?"

"We were parked on the third level of the garage, and she came to get the car after dinner, but she never came back, so I went to look for her and her car's not here. She's gone." Expending all his remaining energy to say these few words, he slumped down to the concrete again.

"I'll come down there right now. Which garage are you in?"

"Next to Chez Toulouse."

Emily assured him, even in the flooded streets, she could get there in her SUV.

Sitting alone, wet and cold, Henry couldn't help but imagine the worst. He could almost see it: Martha, grabbed by a man waiting in the garage, who forced her to drive him to some deserted side street where she was robbed, raped, and murdered. He began to cry, his body shaking.

Fifteen minutes had elapsed when Emily found him still sitting on the concrete deck. Jumping out, she knelt down to help him stand.

"Let's get in my car and you can tell me what happened. We'll figure out what to do."

Henry was glad to have someone tell him what to do. In the car, he recounted the interruption of dinner by Jack Townsend's surprise appearance and his dramatic reaction after being told to leave by Martha.

"You mean the same Jack Townsend that obsessed over Mom for all those years, sending her cards and flowers? The one you all laughed about at the time?"

"The same. He never went away."

"Do you think he might have had something to do with this? I mean, he shows up out of nowhere after all these years, and suddenly Mom disappears?"

"I don't know, Emily." Henry didn't know what to think.

"We should call the police first and report her missing. I'll call 911, and we'll have a cruiser here in minutes. Why don't you call the hotel for any messages? And call George. I'll call Britt. Maybe she's heard something? Then we'll call everyone else."

Henry looked over at Emily.

"Thank you for coming," he said. "I wasn't sure you'd even answer the phone after what was said about me at the college a few hours ago."

"We'll talk later…after we find Mom." She began dialing 911.

Just like her mother, Emily had always been pragmatic and calm when faced with a test or a problem—although not with the same intensity and dedication.

Relieved to have a plan and something constructive to do, Henry began dialing the hotel. There was no answer on the phone in their room, and the front desk did not remember recently seeing her. Henry asked them to please have someone check their room to see if she was in and call him back. He called George Holland, his close friend from the college, but he had not seen or heard from her.

Emily called Britt Pederson, Martha's best friend since high school, who worked at the college in Charleston, but the call went to voicemail. Emily left a detailed message of her mother's disappearance.

A police cruiser arrived. Henry explained the events of the last few hours while giving a description of Martha and the car. The police said they could not formally place her as a missing person until she'd been missing for twenty-four hours but would keep an eye out for her and alert all law enforcement. They advised that he call everyone who knew she was in town today. The police would call Henry with any news or leads but told him it was not uncommon for someone to disappear for a few hours, usually after an argument or disagreement. Henry told them there had been no argument of any kind. The police felt fairly certain she would turn up before long.

Distraught over the news of Martha, Britt called back. She firmly believed she was somehow all right. "Martha has always taken care of herself in any situation," she said, "but I'll also begin searching."

With a new spark of energy, Henry felt himself coming out of his initial fog of despair and inability to function. He asked Emily to drive slowly through the whole parking garage to double check whether the car was parked somewhere else for some reason. It wasn't.

Back at the third level, Emily suggested they put the car's high beams on and scour the deck from wall to wall to look for anything that might be a clue. Henry drove the Tahoe, while Emily checked on foot, aided by her cell phone flashlight. She was searching an empty parking slot between two cars when she turned and waved to Henry. "Come look at this," she yelled.

She was kneeling, looking down at what appeared to be a crushed cell phone.

"Could this be Mom's? It looks like it was a burgundy-colored phone."

An involuntary sharp intake of breath by Henry answered her question. Falling to his knees, he looked at the crushed phone. He was about to pick it up when Emily grabbed his arm. "There may be fingerprints on it and a way to somehow retrieve the information in it. The police know how to handle something like this."

Still on his knees, Henry stared at the phone. "She always had a phone that color." His voice wavered. "Charleston College burgundy. I think Britt has one too." He didn't move from his knees as he stared at the phone.

Minutes later, another police cruiser appeared. Henry explained that he believed it was his wife's phone. The officer carefully gathered up the phone, slipped it into a clear bag, and said that if it was possible to retrieve information, they had a man who could do it.

With nothing more they could do in the garage, and with Emily's SUV, they decided to search the flooded downtown streets. After an hour of circling in the rain, they came up empty.

Emily suggested that they go back to his hotel room and continue to call everyone who might have seen Martha that night or have a sliver of information that would help locate her.

At the hotel, she stopped to drop him off under the front door's overhang before she parked the car. Henry leaned over to her. "I know we'll find her and that she'll be all right," he said. "Your mother is too smart to get in any serious trouble."

He put his hand on her shoulder. "You and I will have a good long talk when we get her back."

He reached up and touched her cheek with the back of his fingers. "But now, let's find your mother." He looked back at her as he got out and saw her eyes filling with tears.

In the room, Henry called room service for snacks. George and Britt stopped by the room after searching on their own. They called everyone they could think of, but no one had seen or heard from Martha. They called hotels to see if she had checked in. Friends called to his room to see if they could do anything, bring anything. Many offered to drive around and just look. The police did not call. They kicked around ideas as to what could happen to Martha that she could go missing just inside of an hour. The air was subdued with no new information. Now that the storm had subsided, they went back out and searched the town again. Exhausted, they parted just past midnight.

Henry walked the deserted bedroom, trying to think of a plausible scenario for what might have happened. He knew it would be unbelievable for Martha to just drive off. Off to where? Why? What the hell is going on? He'd known her for over thirty-five years, and Martha didn't take off and disappear. He tried to think of what could trigger his wife to just leave him standing in front of the restaurant. He walked through the events of the evening in his mind. All was well up until Jack walked in the restaurant. He was there maybe fifteen, twenty minutes, but during that time he…he was, by God, forcing himself on her. Not physically like before, but mentally.

On second thought, although she parried his advances, she did not appear to be offended by them. It was almost as if she took a certain enjoyment, most probably a natural one, in being "sought after"—especially at her age.

On reflection, Henry could understand. He could relate to this middle-age phenomenon.

A month or so before, a tall, exotic Italian grad student had snared him for a few innocent extra hours of English lit help. He had succumbed to the same flattery by a woman some twenty-five years younger than he. It meant nothing to him other than what it was. A young woman had flattered him and seduced him in his office. At the time, he didn't want to face the probable reality that all she wanted was a better grade from him.

He thought about the timing. Jack walked out of the restaurant and no more than ten minutes later, Martha left for the car. He didn't want to think it, but…what if Jack waited just down the street in hopes that by chance, Martha might come out alone to get their car? He could have approached her, talked her into…into what? Henry felt sick to his stomach just thinking of the possibilities. Unable to keep his eyes open any longer, he lay down and fell into a dreamless sleep.

# CHAPTER 4

The following morning at the Third Avenue public boat ramp in downtown Charleston, Robert Chandler and his son, Joey, towing their eighteen-foot Key West, *Lucky Lady*, pulled onto the concrete entrance and stopped. With the sun just breaking the horizon, two city workers, their T-shirts already drenched in sweat, scrambled in front of them, clearing scraps of branches and marsh grass off the parking area and ramp itself, remnants of last night's storm. Scheduled to open at daybreak, and now with the clean-up just about finished, the newly refurbished boat ramp was ready. The wooden-horse barriers—meant to block the entrance during construction—lay on their sides. They had been blown onto the grass, along one side of the entrance, from the storm. Pieces of tattered, yellow *No Trespassing* tape were plastered against them and the surrounding palmetto palms.

As Robert sat in his truck waiting for the workers to finish, he looked at the scene in front of him, out to the Ashley River and the marshes beyond. He rolled down his window. The air was almost cool at that hour. Daybreak had brought clear skies and light winds as last night's storms moved offshore. With most of the humidity being carried away by the storm, the fresh, clean air mingled with the musky smell of the salt marshes, heralding a beautiful day for fishing. With a large grin on his face, he said, "Son, it doesn't get much better than this."

The workers shouted and waved him on that it was clear. Joey jumped out of the truck and climbed on the trailer and onto *Lucky Lady*. Robert eased forward, turned around, and slowly backed the boat down the concrete ramp. Joey hollered him to stop just before the boat began to float off the trailer and started up its 150 Yamaha, leaving it in neutral. Robert put on the parking brake, got out, and walked back to the bow of the boat. Robert grabbed a line that Joey had thrown to him, unhooked the boat, and gave it a shove to free it from the trailer. The boat floated back a few feet before coming to an unexpected stop.

Robert looked back and saw the nose of the boat begin to rotate to its right with the current. He pulled on the line, and the boat came free, drifting slowly downstream in the falling tide. Joey motored back to the dock beside the ramp, where his father waited. Another boat was preparing to launch.

Robert waved them off, yelling, "Better hang on a minute. We just ran into something a little ways down the ramp. It'll be our luck it's a big ol' dead tree trunk that got loose upstream and got stuck right in our way, blocking everything."

He retrieved a mask and snorkel from the boat, along with a waterproof flashlight. He tied a line around his waist and gave the free end to Joey before walking down the ramp into the dark, silt-filled water. When the water reached his waist, he set the mask on his face, flattened out on the surface, and paddled out carefully as the visibility proved limited in the early morning light.

Just ahead, he saw a dark shape that looked like it could be the back end of a car. He paddled up and found a four-door sedan, the top of its roof about a foot below the surface. Paddling to keep his position near the car in the light current, he thought he could make out the shape of a person in the driver's side. Taking a deep breath, he dove down to the open driver's side window and saw a woman sitting in the seat; the interior was flooded, her seat belt holding her in place. A quick look around showed no one else. Robert shot to the surface and yelled, "Call 911! There's a car with a dead woman inside!"

He swam back toward the ramp until he could stand.

He was greeted by a crowd of fishermen gathered around, curious why Robert's pickup still blocked the ramp. Joey could only tell them what his father had shouted out to him. Sirens blared in the distance, closing in toward the boat ramp. Questions rang out as Robert walked up the ramp and Joey met him with a towel.

He wiped his face and head, taking a few deep breaths before he spoke.

"There's a lady in the front seat of the car, still buckled in. No one else. The car is full of water. She's dead. We'd better not touch anything until the police and EMS get here."

He turned to Joey, whose face had turned pale. He looked as if he was about to get sick. Putting his arm around him, Robert said, "Son, why don't you go get in the truck and sit down for a spell. We'll figure out what to do here. I'll be back in a jiffy."

The questions flew at Robert from all directions. He had to wave his hands to get them to stop.

"There's no tellin' how she got to be there. I mean, how do you drive down a ramp until you're under water?"

The arrival of a fire truck, the EMS, and two police cars quieted the crowd. The various responders assembled around Robert while he offered a detailed account—covering the time they arrived at the ramp until he emerged from the water. The police cleared the boat ramp area of all boaters, except for Robert and Joey, and set the wooden-horse barriers up to block the entrance.

First into the water was the fire department dive team, loaded down with air tanks, masks, cameras, lights, and radios. The divers circled the car taking photos while giving a recorded report to the responders on land of what they were seeing. Approaching the car, they took photos of Martha and the vehicle's flooded interior.

The dive team came out of the water, reporting to the police that there was a middle-aged woman still buckled in her seat belt, sitting in the driver's seat—apparently dead. No one else was inside. The car was filled with water with both front windows open. There were no obvious damages to the car, which was a dark blue or black four-door sedan with a North Carolina license plate. The police confirmed it was the tag number of the car reported missing last evening by a Professor Willis.

"Well, it must have happened sometime last night during the storm," commented one of the policemen. "And Mr. Chandler and his son were the first here, at daybreak, when they found it."

A tow truck winched the car out of the water. The body was transferred to an EMS truck. After the remaining water inside the car drained out, the police inspected the car. A purse laying on the floorboard of the passenger's side contained a wallet and various ID cards, identifying her as Martha Willis, professor, Southern College. They noted that her wallet contained eighty-three dollars in cash, as well as various family photos and credit cards. A single umbrella lay in the backseat, along with what appeared to be a seat belt for a small pet of some sort.

After inspecting Robert's boat and reviewing Robert and Joey's original statements, they thanked them for their help and said they would be back in touch soon.

With his arm draped around Joey's shoulders, Robert said, "Son, let's pack up and go home. There's nothing more we can do here."

"Dad," said Joey, as they walked back to the truck, "how does something like this happen? I mean, we came down here to go fishing and look at what we found! A dead woman, sitting in a car, underwater. I don't know what to think. I don't know if I'll be able to go fishing again without thinking about this." He lay his head against his father's wide chest.

"I wish you hadn't seen this. I don't have an explanation for what happened." He hugged him. "We'll go home and talk about it with Mom."

They moved one of the barriers at the entrance and drove off just as the sun was beginning to clear the tree line.

————

It was 8:30 a.m. and Henry was sleeping soundly after being up most of the night. He had collapsed around 3:00 a.m. with no news.

He was awakened by a knocking on his door. He found his bathrobe and stumbled to the door. A policeman stood with his hat in hand. The look on his face told Henry what he feared most.

"Mr. Henry Willis?" asked the policeman.

"Yes," he whispered, feeling his knees begin to buckle.

"May I come in?"

"Yes." He stepped back and almost fell. He sat on the edge of the bed, staring at the policeman and hoping this was a dream.

"I'm sorry to have to tell you this, but your wife was found drowned in her car just after daybreak this morning. The car was underwater at the end of the Third Street boat ramp. We assume it went into the water sometime last night. Her seat belt was still buckled. No other person found in the car with her and no signs of a struggle or obvious cuts or bruises that would indicate she had been attacked in some way. There will be an investigation into the accident and an autopsy will be performed to confirm the cause of death, as well as the approximate time."

Henry heard little of what he said after the first sentence.

————

Henry was driven to the police station and then the morgue to identify Martha. It was the hardest undertaking of his life. Overwhelmed, he nearly collapsed, and he was led away and taken to a seat. He was in shock and could not assemble his thoughts in any order other than trying to digest what he had just seen. He couldn't accept that she was dead. There must be a mistake. He had been cast adrift, alone in a lifeboat. She had so much to live for. His head dropped, and he wept. He was given a ride back to his hotel.

After the police left, Henry had a rental car delivered to the hotel. He drove to Emily's apartment, hoping he had the emotional strength to tell her. He rang the doorbell and waited with tears running down his cheeks. She opened the door, looked at him, and murmured, "Oh no…oh no!" She fell, leaning against the door jamb.

Henry put his arm around her, and they held each other. "She's dead," was all he could manage to say. "She drove down a boat ramp by mistake and into the river. The car sunk before she could get out. She was found a few hours ago."

He managed to walk her to the sofa, where they both collapsed in each other's arms. Emily sat up slowly and stared out the window that faced the courtyard. He could see her jaw tighten and her head shake almost imperceptibly. He knew what she was thinking, that he should have gone with her to the garage in those stormy conditions. But I didn't. I had hesitated, just like I had with my son, Phillip. Now Martha is lost to Emily and me.

Henry had said the same words to himself, suddenly feeling as if every thread of life had been pulled from him.

# CHAPTER 5

The funeral would be held at the small brick church, with its simple white steeple, which stood in a wooded glen of tall hardwoods close to the campus of Southern College outside Asheville. A light rain had started that morning, the low clouds mirroring Henry's mood. He still harbored a resentment for Charleston's hot, thick air, and storm-force winds and rain that had taken his wife to her death in a dark river. He stood outside his home, not a half mile from the church. For a moment, the cool, pure mountain breeze from the north tempered his grief. Over the past week, he had succumbed to having a drink in the early afternoon in his study. Most days, wine and cognac supplanted a large portion of his normal intake of calories from food. To some extent, his health and mental state had deteriorated accordingly.

The initial investigation concluded in part that Martha Willis had driven down the boat ramp by mistake in the rainstorm. The car submerged so quickly that she was unable to free herself from her seat belt and drowned. There was no sign of any foul play, or any other person having been in the car. After talking with Henry concerning Martha's state of mind that night, the police eliminated suicide as a possibility. The investigation would continue, and an autopsy performed, but the preliminary investigation concluded there was no evidence to suggest anything other than an unfortunate accident.

Overcome with grief, Henry tried to make some sense of this. His wife had just been snatched from him in a bizarre mishap. Something was not right, but Henry could not be sure of anything, and now he had to face the funeral. He wished he didn't have to mix with the many friends and faculty, accepting their condolences. That much close social interaction unnerved him, so he took refuge in his house the morning of the funeral. He needed another drink and some company, so he called George—head of the college drama department and his only real friend—and asked if he would join him.

His study smelled of wood smoke, leather-bound books, burnished floors, and the faint scent of tobacco. They sat in the study in the leather armchairs surrounded by walls of well-worn books and sipped coffee in silence, comforted by the familiar room that had hosted so many discussions between them. Finally, Henry broke the silence in a low voice.

"George, I don't know what to think, what to do. I've lost Martha, and I know Emily is upset and disheartened with me again for my involvement in another death in our family. She has every right to be, you know."

"Henry, you can't blame yourself for these accidents."

But Henry disagreed. These were avoidable accidents and he had to replay them out loud.

"First, it was our son, Phillip, in college and having trouble with drugs and depression. He called on a Friday afternoon for us to come see him. But I dithered about in my flower garden, even with Martha urging me to move along, to get going, until it was too late to drive to Chapel Hill. We would go the next morning." He stopped and gathered himself, wiping his eyes. Just above a whisper, his voice cracked as he said, "Phillip overdosed that Friday night." He stood and walked to the window, staring out at the rain. Turning, he shuffled back to his chair and slumped down. "A week ago, I stayed to pay the check at the restaurant and let Martha go alone for the car in the storm. Such simple inactions on my part."

Standing, George walked over beside Henry and put his hand on his shoulder.

"Henry, sometimes life can paralyze us if we dwell too long on unfortunate accidents of life that we have no control over. But for now, we'd better head over to the church."

It took all of Henry's strength to rise from the chair and make it out the front door.

———

Martha's service began at two o'clock and the church was filled. Everyone from the college and all those from Charleston who had been a part of their lives were present. Unable to travel, Henry's mother had sent her condolences. As always, his father remained silent. Martha's high school friends were there, many of whom, along with Martha, had been presented together into Charleston society at the debutante ball. Henry spotted Martha's widowed mother, Nancy Davis, for the first time since their wedding. Nancy, who imagined herself the touchstone of social life in Charleston, had let it be known that she had been disappointed that her daughter was marrying Henry Willis. Later, he learned that she had told someone at their wedding that Martha deserved better than a poor preacher's son from Cool Springs, wherever that was, and knew she would leave him before the first year was out. He had not spoken to her since and was relieved when she sent word that she would not be speaking to him today. That was fine with him.

Henry sat silently beside Emily and was moved by the many eloquent remembrances of Martha. Britt gave one of the most stirring tributes to her that brought tears to him and most everyone in the church. After the service, the congregation braved the now heavy downpour to gather at the burial plot.

Henry made his way to the tent where the simple wood coffin waited. As he walked up the rows filled with friends, he spotted her in the front row and his heart leaped. For a second, he thought it was Martha, that she was alive, and they were at someone else's funeral. It surprised him to see Emily sitting there. She had not seen him yet and the seat remained open, reserved for him. He was not sure he had the strength to watch his wife buried and face their daughter after her renewed silence toward him. He walked up and sat down. Taking a slow, deep breath, he reached over and took her hand. Looking straight ahead, tears made their way down his face again. They sat this way until the service ended, and they were the only two left.

"What are you going to do now?" asked Emily. "As it turned out, your affair became merely a footnote to the evening, considering how it ended." She stopped, looking away. When she turned back to him, she said, "Twice now, you've become distracted by something inconsequential, hesitated, and it's led to a death in our family."

Although he tried, Henry had no answer.

"Emily, your mother forgave me for the one indiscretion in my life. It was a one-night mistake that had never happened before. I have to try and live with myself for not going with her to get the car." He stopped for a moment. "And not a day goes by that I don't think of our son. These are burdens that I'll carry the rest of my life."

She turned back toward him. "She was your wife, your intellectual mirror, the one who held you up when you didn't think you could stand." She stopped, glaring at the still-moist dirt covering her mother.

Henry's shoulders slumped. He wanted to lie down on top of the dirt, melt into the ground, and join her.

"I have to drive back to Charleston today," she said. "I have a paper to present the day after tomorrow." She stood and stared at the grave until looking over at Henry, and her voice softened. "Would you like to go to the house, have a coffee, and talk?"

He stared a moment, his eyes welling. "I would like that very much, Emily," he croaked.

She smiled. "I'll meet you there," she said and walked away.

As Henry turned to leave, his eye caught the sight of a man standing at the edge of the woods that bordered the cemetery. The rain had backed off to a steady drizzle, and as Henry bent over to open his umbrella, he glanced back toward the woods. Though the man wore a black raincoat and dark hat pulled down covering part of his face, Henry thought he recognized Jack Townsend.

Henry quickly turned away, shutting his eyes tightly for a moment. With his head down, he strode toward his car. I must be mistaken, he thought, although he suddenly found it hard to breathe. He was all but panting when he reached the safety of his car. He turned back and looked to find him, but he was gone.

He met Emily at the house and suggested they sit in the study. Emily refused, insisting that they sit in the kitchen.

"Let's sit in Mother's room, not yours."

"Mother spent a lot of time in the study," said Henry.

"She did, but it was always *your* room."

Henry sat down at the breakfast table. He felt much more comfortable and in control when in his study. He had never thought of it that way, but Emily was right. This room was Martha's. Her territory. And here he was, in a most likely difficult conversation with his thirty-two-year-old daughter. A daughter he was all but estranged from since Phillip's death and their uneasy silence that followed.

She made two coffees and set them down on the table. They sat a moment staring at each other over the rims of their cups as they tested the heat of the coffee.

"I'm sorry I spoke so harshly to you at the gravesite," Emily said. "I shouldn't ever have forgotten the road you had to take to be sitting here now." Her next words surprised him for they had never talked of this before. "Some years back, I asked Mom why you were quieter, more respectful to her than most of the other fathers I knew were to their wives. She said it was all related to an incident in high school that changed your temperament, your character. When she met you in college, you were so withdrawn that it was a struggle to get you into a conversation and to finally explain what had happened in high school. You beating up an innocent boy in a cross-country race who you thought had tripped you on purpose. Apparently, you were quite the tough guy back in the day. When you were called Hank."

"Since that day, I've been Henry, my real name, a different person," he said softly.

"You sent that boy to the hospital, and you never recovered completely from your trauma of that day. Thankfully, your studies and your intellect gave you direction and a scholarship to Chapel Hill. Mom told me your father, the preacher, was so embarrassed by your beating that boy, he all but kept you in your room and shamed you into submission."

Henry shut his eyes. As his head dropped, he shook his head. He looked up.

"Those were the worst months of my young life," he said in a hoarse voice. "I wrote the boy letters apologizing but they were all returned, unopened, and I haven't seen or talked to him since."

"Mom told me she met you at an English lit conference in Charleston when you were seniors. She saw something special in you and took you under her wing, even though I've been told that she had the pick of most any rich, handsome boy in Charleston. She rescued you, became your guardian. And after college, she took you both away from the social strata of Charleston to a smaller town in the mountains. Where you both would have space to make your lives on your own abilities, and not on your connections."

Reaching out, she covered his hand with hers.

"I know you realize you should have gone to the garage with her, and I know why you didn't. She probably overrode you when you offered to go with her, didn't she?"

He looked off, remembering that moment. "Yes, she did," he whispered.

Emily said, "She'd been your protector for so long that you had become dependent on her. You trusted her, and in the end, she knew what was best. I think your hesitation to act in certain decisions has been ingrained in you since high school. You don't trust your instincts and Mom never pushed you to be more than you desired."

Henry nodded. "I know that, Emily." He was lost and knew it. He looked at her, his eyes moist. "What am I going to do, Emily?"

"I don't have the answer. You either go in your study and slowly wither away, or you stand up and do something Mother would be proud of. Maybe something not related to English literature?"

To Henry, she might as well have suggested he become an astronaut. He was out of words.

She squeezed his hand.

"I've got to go," she said, walking around behind him and giving him a hug and a kiss on his cheek. Taking her umbrella, she walked out into the rain. Henry stood and walked to his study, watching her through the window with misty eyes. She had surprised him with her perception. He then noticed a red sports car parked just down the street. An uncommon car for the neighborhood. Just as Emily drove off, the car pulled out and passed by slowly. He thought he recognized Jack Townsend behind the wheel.

# CHAPTER 6

Henry had been "old" for some time without even realizing it—a gray man in a gray world—an overweight professor with little self-confidence outside the academic arena. His small circle of academic friends fed on each other's intellectualism. His required attendance at a football game each year, which he considered a gladiatorial type event, unnerved him, and he was thankful to retreat back to his book-laden study and the comfort it brought. He had been existing in a self-contained cocoon administered by Martha, the one who had rescued him from his old life.

Retired from the college, he retreated completely into his house. His only company now was his dog Falstaff, an old basset hound who was content to sleep at his feet most of the day. With the heavy curtains closed, he set up pictures of Martha around the study, lit candles, drank wine and cognac, and talked to her. From time to time, he would take a drive, top down, in his restored red MG-TD with Falstaff beside him; they traveled through wooded hills on two-lane roads in the clear mountain air. He found it was the only time he could escape his grief for a few moments. But soon, it would remind him of his and Martha's plans upon retirement. They would go to the English countryside for an extended stay and visit the historical areas of old England that they had studied, dreaming about for so long. They would drive in a red convertible with the top down, the wind in their hair. He would return to his study and stare at the old, enlarged photograph of a couple riding in a red Jaguar XKE with the top down that he and Martha had found in an old bookstore some years before while driving in the English countryside. This is what they would do when they retired. But this memory only lifted him for a fleeting moment before the dark clouds of grief engulfed him again.

Henry's depression deepened. In the end, he knew that Jack Townsend was to blame. He was the catalyst for all that had happened: his provocative suggestions toward Martha, her telling him to leave and his explosive response, her third glass of wine, abandoning dinner, Martha leaving alone to get the car. Jack Townsend precipitated the downward spiral of their evening, culminating in his wife's tragic drowning. Who could have foreseen such a confluence of seemingly disparate events resulting in her death?

"Goddamn him," he muttered between clenched teeth.

Martha was gone and his life had flatlined. Food and medications were delivered to the house. For a while, his few friends and various faculty members stopped by to visit but found Henry all but nonresponsive. Worried, they sent his pastor and then his doctor to visit. They prayed and prescribed more medication. Even George, his one true friend for the past thirty years, could not crack the shell Henry had crawled into.

It had been weeks since he buried Martha, and he felt himself sliding into an abyss with no idea of how to escape. He returned to his therapist for counseling. She had helped him through his traumatic experience in high school, then again after Phillip's death, then on and off with his problem communicating with Emily. And now for Martha.

He shook his head and stood. I have to get the ship righted. A small point, or item, from the police report bothered him, and he couldn't quite bring it into focus. He slowly walked around the dimly lit room, forcing himself to think of what he was told or shown by them. Finally, there it was.

"It was her purse!" he said aloud before sitting back down. The police gave the purse back to him and said it was found on the floor in front of the passenger's seat. They showed him the photo. It didn't register with him at the time, and the police had no reason to question it. But now, he remembered she *always* set her purse beside her left leg when she was driving—*always*. She was too methodical in her habits. She would have placed it on her side, to her left, without thinking—a reflex action. Someone had to have moved it over there. His eyes widened at this thought. My God, she was murdered! Henry then recalled Emily's final words to him, "Do something Martha would be proud of."

A most unlikely thought came to him. Since the police had ruled this an accident and had no more interest in the case, maybe *he* could track down the person who killed his wife. No investigators. No police. No professionals. Just by myself. He had no idea how he would go about such an endeavor, but the thought of seeking revenge triggered a new feeling in him, one he didn't recognize. It was a feeling, not of excitement, but more of need. The need that he *had* to do *something.* A feeling of anticipation came over him. His thinking then floundered and he became frozen by the thought. Revenge to what extent? At this moment, he could not dwell on specifics, but he found this thought gave his thinking a direction, a purpose.

He was fifty-six, a retired English professor, and had no clue what to do. Henry poured another glass of wine, sat in his armchair, leaned back, and lit his briarwood pipe. For a moment, he felt safe, ensconced in his study, surrounded by books. The chill of loneliness and emptiness quickly washed over him.

He called George and asked if he would stop by when he had a chance.

———

George rang the doorbell after lunch. Henry poured two glasses of wine before settling down in the worn leather armchairs.

"Henry, you look like hell," said George with a smile.

"Thank you. I feel like hell." Henry raised his glass. "George, you know me better than anyone I know, maybe even better, in some instances, than

Martha. I've got an idea, and it's so far outside my comfort zone, my character, that I wanted to run it by you." He took a sip of wine. "To be sure I haven't slipped over the edge."

"Okay, Henry, I'm sitting."

"I believe Jack Townsend killed Martha, and I'm going to get him."

Leaning forward, George carefully set his glass down.

"Avenge her death? I understood it was an accident. There must be more to it than you've told me."

"Yes, yes, there is. I've told you about Jack Townsend, the jet pilot who followed Martha over the years with cards and flowers. Well, when we were at Chez Toulouse that last night, Jack suddenly appeared, invited himself for a drink, and blatantly flattered Martha until she finally told him to stop it and 'leave, forever.' That's when he exploded, jumped up, and knocked over drinks, saying that nobody gives *him* orders. He roared off, almost knocking over the maître d' and stormed out the door. It was both shocking and embarrassing and, needless to say, dinner was ruined. Martha left shortly afterward to get the car." He paused, shaking his head. "In the end, I believe that Jack Townsend is responsible for her death. He was there and had the opportunity. My God, he followed and tracked her for over thirty years. He was obsessed with her. And Martha's purse was found on the passenger's side floor. Martha always put it by her left leg when she was driving. Whoever killed her moved it."

"I have to admit," said George, "you may have a point. From what you've told me of the investigation, though, it was ruled an accident with no sign of anyone having been in the car except Martha. If Jack was not in the car, and knowing Martha, it's doubtful he could have somehow upset her enough to lose control and drive herself into the river."

Henry nodded.

"Yes, someone had to have been in the car besides Martha when the car went in the river."

Silence enveloped the room. Henry opened his eyes, staring. He sat up.

"Even if I had seen him kill her, taking revenge and an eye for an eye attitude might salve my wounds for a moment, but it would be wrong. And against the law. I would end up in jail or driving myself into the river."

He paused a moment, staring at his friend.

"I'll prove he killed her and let justice take its course. I must not lose the opportunity to prove myself to Emily, the only family I have." His eyes moistened. "The only family she has."

Rising from his chair, Henry walked over to the bookshelves lining the wall. He reached up and touched a book, and then slowly wandered along, trailing his finger along the row of books. He glanced at titles of famous works that he had taught over the years. His finger stopped at a small leather-bound book, titled *Hamlet* by William Shakespeare. He lost himself in thought for a moment as he pondered Hamlet's quest to avenge the death of his father.

He turned back to the room.

"George, I'll follow in Hamlet's footsteps. It will be in keeping with my life's study."

He walked back, sat down, and sipped his wine.

"If I learn Jack Townsend was complicit in some way in her death, then I will go forward." He stared off for what seemed like minutes. "He took something from me that I loved very much," he said. "I will see that he loses what *he* cherishes most. What do you think?"

George took a sip of wine and studied Henry.

"That's an ambitious undertaking for someone like you. You'd be stepping into an arena you know nothing about and have no training in." He stopped a moment. "The odds are not with you, my friend."

"George, I have nothing else I *need* to do, or *must* do, more in my life right now!"

"I have a suggestion before you strap on a six-shooter and ride into town. What about a short test run to see if it's even in you, mentally, to investigate a person undercover? Find where this Jack Townsend lives, go there, and learn something about the man from another person—all without raising any suspicions or causing you any danger."

Henry thought on this a moment. He had acted in the drama club in college. If there remains an ounce of acting in my body, maybe I can do such a thing. If not, and he collapsed on stage, doing no more than what George suggested, he had no business signing up for this revenge undertaking. "You're right. That would be the smart thing to do." He sat staring off at nothing.

George stood. "Give me a call when you decide what to do and I'll back you up anyway I can." He patted Henry's shoulder.

"Thank you," Henry mumbled, lost in thought about what he had decided to do. What he *must* do. He would avenge Martha, and it would be subtle, something only a professor with a PhD in English literature could imagine. He was to be a gladiator in his own way, and the thought almost made him faint. He steeled himself, stood, and walked deliberately to the windows where he opened all the curtains.

# CHAPTER 7

Henry turned on his laptop and typed in *Jack Townsend, Air Carolinas pilot,* and a short paragraph popped up: *Born in Charleston, South Carolina, age forty-nine, college at The Citadel, navy flight school, carrier pilot in the Middle East, discharged from the navy, pilot for Southern Air, Airways Atlantic, and presently Air Carolinas. Now living in Charleston, South Carolina, home base for Air Carolinas.*

He's bounced around a lot since the navy, thought Henry. His address is 286-A Meeting Street in Charleston.

———

In the morning, Henry drove to Charleston with no idea of what he would do. But he did know where Jack lived and that was all he needed for now.

He checked in at a Holiday Inn downtown, shed his coat and tie for more casual attire, put on a floppy hat, and walked to the welcome center to get a detailed map of the city. He didn't trust trying to follow the GPS directions on his phone. Besides, a large paper map gave him a sense of the layout of the city and a place to make notes. Old school works best for me.

Jack's address was three blocks away on Meeting Street, and he decided to walk down for a look. Summer came early to Charleston and the grass had turned green; the azaleas were beginning to bloom. A morning shower had cut the humidity, and Henry found a little bounce in his step as he headed out on his first investigative excursion.

He quickly found the address behind a historic, three-story, brick Charleston house with its narrow front facing the street with open air porches on all floors along its right side. Beside it ran a narrow driveway, lined with crepe myrtle trees that led to a small parking area in the rear. Henry walked down the drive, hoping Jack was not around. Attached to the rear of the main house was a smaller two-story house, which appeared to be split into two units with copper letters *A* and *B* tacked on the two front doors. There were no cars in any of the parking spaces and no activity. Walking back to the front of the house, Henry spotted the Coffee Café directly across the street. It was squeezed in between an insurance agency and a ladies clothing store. He crossed over, went in, and noticed a scattering of late breakfast customers toward the back.

He took a seat at a small table by the window, which looked straight down the driveway. The attractive waitress walked over with a cheerful smile, her black hair pulled back in a ponytail. He ordered a coffee and a doughnut.

When his coffee arrived, he added three packs of sugar and two helpings of cream to produce a caramel-colored sweet liquid.

Spreading out his map, he marked his hotel and unit A. He was pleased with himself for this progress—after only two hours in town. He looked over the top of the paper to check the driveway. All was quiet. He felt like he was in a B movie, sitting behind a storefront and sipping coffee on stakeout. All he needed was smoke rising up around him from a Camel cigarette.

Henry signaled the waitress over and, much to his own surprise, slipped into his new movie role almost without thinking. "I've just arrived in town and may possibly try renting for a spell, before committing on where I might stay on a more permanent basis. Do you happen to know any of the people who live across the street?"

"The owners of the big house come by occasionally," she reported, "and the pilot in A stops by whenever he's in town."

Henry put the paper down. He wanted to ask questions about the pilot in A but thought he should be more circumspect.

"The units in back, are they part of the original house?"

"Oh yes. The house is over two hundred years old. The units in back were the original kitchen and stable for the house. Years ago, they were converted into apartments, or carriage houses. The owners rent them out, long term mostly."

Henry realized he might be spending a lot of time here in this chair following Jack, and added, "By the way, my name is Arthur." He despised lying but thought of himself as an actor. He thought it appropriate that he had played Hamlet on his college stage.

She smiled. "I'm Sally. Nice to meet you, Arthur."

"Could you give me the name of the owners across the way? I just may want to check on the availability of a unit, the amount of the rent, and minimum length of term."

"Why, sure. Be right back." She walked to the counter and was back in a minute. "Here you go," she said, "don't have their phone number, though. Best thing is to just knock on the door. They're real nice folks."

"Thanks, Sally, that's a big help. Did you say the guy in unit A is a pilot? That has to be an interesting and exciting profession."

"It must be by the stories Jack—that's his name—tells me. When he comes in here, I mean. He flies for Air Carolinas," she said, smiling as if *she* were proud of him. She looked around, a little embarrassed by what she'd said.

"I've always thought a profession like a pilot or a salesman, where you're on the road…or the sky, I should say, all the time would be hard on a marriage," said Henry, probing for more information.

"Oh, he's not married anymore. He's lives by himself in A." She looked out toward the driveway. "He's a real charmer, he is."

Henry gave her his best smile. "Sally, do I detect a little interest in the pilot in A?"

Blushing, she shook her head. "It's just that he's asked me out a few times." In a nervous gesture, she brushed at her skirt, diverting her gaze from Henry.

Henry did not want to push any farther. He had learned more than he had hoped.

"Well, I must be going. I've taken more of your time than I deserved."

Standing, he put the map into his pocket. Taking a ten-dollar bill from his wallet, he placed it into her hand.

"Sally, you're the first person I've had a conversation with since arriving in Charleston. I hope any other conversation I have is half as charming as this one has been." He put on his hat, put his finger to the brim, nodded, and left.

Upon reflection, Henry thought his stop at the coffee shop and asking questions about the rental units across the street with the waitress who knew the pilot may have been too direct. The pilot was most probably in town and if he stopped by the coffee shop, Sally might well mention there was someone looking to rent unit B. The pilot would want to know what type of person was looking, as they could become neighbors. Sally could give a very good description of him. It would be a stretch, but Jack might connect the description as possibly being Henry Willis. Although he wasn't sure why, this realization sent a chill through him.

His elation over finding out so much about Jack in the first hours in Charleston was short lived. The more he thought about it, the more he realized he wasn't even up to grade as a B movie spook. He needed to stop and think over this whole operation he was considering. A place that surrounded him with comfort had always helped clear his head, a place for rumination. He found it on Calhoun Street, two blocks over from Meeting Street. The Charleston County Library, a three-story brick building that covered almost a block. He walked up the slate stairs to the information desk and was directed to the reading room. He found an empty table, sat down, and exhaled. He was home…away from home.

Removing his yellow legal pad from his leather carrying bag, he began making notes of everything he knew about Jack Townsend and specifically what was said at the restaurant with Martha that night. He made a list of what reports on the accident might be available, including lists of possible witnesses he could talk to: from the man who discovered the sunken car to anyone outside the restaurant to possible people around the parking garage who might have seen her.

Henry couldn't help himself and his thinking veered off course into what he would really like to do to the pilot if he found him guilty. Shoot him? Maybe cause an "accident" and run over him? Tie him up in a car and shove it into the river? Take a sword and run him through? When he caught himself, he stopped and took a deep breath. This was not his intended method of revenge. This was not the professor speaking. His emotions were overruling his brain. He wondered if this was Henry Willis that was making the dark list. Can I sign my name at the bottom of it, declaring, yes, Henry Willis wrote this?

Shaken, he stood up and leaned on the desk. He needed air. Looking around the room, he was worried that anyone nearby would somehow know what he had written and was now calling 911. He snatched off the page with the list, folded it repeatedly, and stuffed it into his pocket. Sitting back down, he looked closely at the blank sheet that was below the list and remembered something he saw on TV or a movie. From the indentations, he could make out most of the words. He tore it off and was about to throw the list and blank sheet in the trash can when he saw the police retrieving the evidence. My God, he'd have to burn everything. He packed everything back in his bag and hurried from the room, glancing back to see how many people were watching him. All heads were down, but he knew they had been watching him.

Henry made his way back to the hotel and to his room. Exhausted, he felt short of breath. The room was warm with the afternoon sun beaming through the window. He closed the curtain, turned down the thermostat, went in the bathroom, and threw cold water on his face. He fished his heart pills and high blood pressure pills from his pocket and drank a glass of water. Looking in the mirror, he didn't recognize who he saw. Red faced and puffy, hair standing out from his ears, eyes wide. A Halloween clown came to mind. He stumbled back to the bed and collapsed on his back, his heart racing.

# CHAPTER 8

Henry awoke the next morning after a restless night. The previous evening, he decided that it would be best if he didn't show his face on the streets of Charleston, imagining Jack knew he was in town, so he had dined from the room service menu and sipped hotel cabernet until he dozed off. Because Jack Townsend knew what he looked like, and if he was going to "tail" him, the first thing he must do is change his appearance. He could no longer look and talk like a professor of English literature if he was going to become…a spy, a sleuth? It scared him to just think of the words. But how would one go about doing such a thing? Then it came to him. He called the drama department at the college and asked for his friend George.

"Hello, Henry," said George, "how are you holding up?"

"I'm still standing, but it's not any easier. George, I wanted to ask a favor."

"Of course, anything I can do."

"Don't think I'm crazy, but it will take me a minute to explain. I need to change who I am…for two reasons. The first is practical: to investigate the pilot, I can't look like I do. The second is more psychological. The need to escape out of the stupor of sorrow that engulfs me and overcome my obvious ineptness in engaging socially outside academia." He paused. "I feel if I try being someone else for a while, someone I don't recognize, then maybe the sorrow will fade and I can gain the confidence to continue on, to look at life through a new lens. I believe it's the only way I can have a chance of succeeding in this venture. I must become somebody I'm not. And I thought maybe you could help me do this. We've worked together on productions, and I have watched how you make a college junior become a young Hamlet. Can you make an old fart like me into someone like an older Hamlet?"

"Henry, that's what I do, and I will do everything I can to help you through this. I've known you and Martha for thirty years, and I know how close to her you were and what she meant to you. Your idea for recovery, I find, is really quite interesting." He paused for a moment. "And I think a therapist would find it…innovative. You could become someone else for a while and view your experience and loss through new eyes. It could thrust you to look at new ideas and territories of pursuit that you never imagined. You may live another twenty or thirty years and find a whole new calling. Who knows who Henry Willis might become? By God, it's an exciting thought!"

Hearing this scenario from a close friend, Henry was equally excited. George had added a whole new layer to Henry's original reason for changing his appearance. He couldn't wait to begin the transformation.

"George, if you have the time, I'd like to start right away. I'm in Charleston right now, but I'm heading back today. Could I stop by tomorrow? Is that too soon? If it is, I'll just wait till you're free."

"We just finished our spring production of *Othello* and everything is sliding to a halt with summer school upon us. Come on home and we'll get started."

"Thank you. I'll owe you a case of cognac."

———

Henry was eager to be on the road, ready to become the *new* Henry. The idea of what he was going to do, what he might become, both thrilled and terrified him. These two emotions had been absent from his being for longer than he could remember.

He knew one thing he had to do was lose weight. That morning, he began before he left. At the breakfast buffet at the hotel, normally he would have had eggs, bacon, and hash browns with a muffin on the side. Instead, he had yogurt and a banana. By the time he checked out and got on the road, he was hungry. He worked on putting this out of his mind. If he was to be a new person, he knew it would not come easy. A new mental and physical challenge confronted him. But it felt refreshing to at last be focused with the beginning of a plan. Martha would be aghast to know what he was about to do but knowing her, he felt she would also be proud of him.

He arrived at the college soon after lunch and went by his house to check on the mail. Other than notes of condolence cards from friends, the mail was the same as it had been for decades. He opened all the curtains and windows to let in the fresh spring air and aroma of the jasmine beside the house. Even in his grief, he somehow felt renewed with purpose. He felt this must be how early explorers setting sail for the New World must have felt when they weighed anchor and pointed their small, fragile ships west, knowing not what lay ahead. "Henry the Professor" would become "Henry the Navigator" and discoverer of new lands.

"George," said Henry as he walked into the drama department, "I'm back and ready for the production to begin."

"Well, I must say, you look excited. Grab a chair and I'll get us some coffee." As he brought the coffee, he said, "I take it you felt the trip was a success."

"Overall, I'd say it was. But I quickly learned that one must be completely immersed in his character and quick on his feet to have any success without being detected."

"Yes, I imagine so," said George. "In conversations, there's no room for hesitation or stuttering about. They'll all be in 'real time,' not rehearsed for weeks beforehand as we do here," said George.

"I was in a little coffee café across the street from where the pilot lives for about twenty minutes talking to the waitress pretending to be someone I wasn't. I managed to get some valuable information and was proud of myself for my performance. After leaving, it occurred to me that I talked like a professor, looked like a professor, and dressed like one. Any mention of me by the waitress to Townsend and he'll know who was there. I have to say, it was all a bit unnerving."

"But you're determined to proceed, I gather."

"Most definitely."

"I've been thinking about how best to dress you up. No more smoking a pipe in a tweed coat with portions of this morning's breakfast clinging to your sweater. Maybe a few different styles if you need to change the look from time to time. You could be a typical blue-collar tourist, a middle management type from town, or an artsy type for the opera or a painting auction. Someone your age could be all of these. If you study the habits, speech, and mannerisms, you could pass as one of these characters superficially. If not subject to deep inspection, that is…"

"I could try to become those people and perhaps be believable, but they're a long way from who I am." Henry sipped on his coffee, then put the cup down and stared off in the distance a moment. "You know, George, this whole idea scares the shit out of me."

A smile spread across George's face. "Henry, hearing you put it that way gives me hope that we can get control of your professorial instincts."

"I need to become a new person, the opposite of me, that I can be comfortable being, someone that I have confidence in for conversing and asking questions of strangers in Charleston. And who doesn't sound like a professor interrogating them."

"Someone like Falstaff?"

"Ah, of course. A jovial person you'd like to sit and have a beer with and yet not realize how much information he's getting out of you." He chuckled at the thought. "And doesn't seem out of place in Charleston." He frowned.

Suddenly, George blurted out, "A tourist! They're all over Charleston, asking questions, stumbling around trying to find their way."

"By God, I like it. Let's get started."

"I can take lessons from Falstaff!" said Henry excitedly.

"Yes, your basset hound, Falstaff, can make you laugh, make you shake your head in frustration, but somehow always seems to get his way."

"Okay, here's an important thing that you need to learn. Most men, in any profession, talk sports. It's the common language of the male species. So, begin by reading the sports pages, another new adventure. And I'll give you some new reading material to study." He smiled. "You'll be quizzed on all this, every day."

Henry blinked. "I haven't taken a test in decades."

"It'll be easier than transforming your professor's body. When do you get on with that?"

"I start training tomorrow down at the Forum. Fat off, muscle on, as they like to say. We'll see if they can remold this old overweight geezer."

"It should be fun." George chuckled. "I doubt you've ever done a push up in your life."

# CHAPTER 9

Henry jumped into his physical and mental transformation with an eagerness that surprised him. From reconnoitering Jack's apartment at the coffee shop to now changing his appearance for up-close undercover work, he had not merely slipped out of his box but jumped out. He found all this both terrifying and exhilarating.

The most difficult of tasks came first—losing weight. He had joined the Fitness Forum in town and asked the personal trainer to shape him up. After a few days at the Forum, he feared he might die before he got to Jack Townsend. The new diet, the weights, the self-defense course, and spinning were activities he could not imagine anyone doing voluntarily. But what he dreaded most were the days when he would have opted for the lions in the Roman Forum rather than another session at the Fitness Forum with Buster Lloyd and the heavy bag. He had sworn off hitting anything with his fists since the incident in high school, but for Martha he would make an exception. He pushed it from his mind, realizing he would need to rekindle some of the tenacity and confidence he had been missing for nearly thirty-five years. The force he used to hit the bag rattled his body more than any other item in his regimen, other than giving up wine and cognac. But each evening when he retired to his study with a bottle of Power Boost, surrounded by pictures of him and Martha, he braced himself for another day.

George had also set Henry up with an optometrist, men's hair salon, conferences with a private investigator, attorney, police captain, and a forensic pathologist. He even sent him to a men's store for a new wardrobe.

There was also the difficult question of Henry's speech pattern, which George took on to correct. "Henry, although you were born and raised in North Carolina, you've been an English professor for twenty-five years or so, and you talk like one. You also have an interesting habit you've acquired over time. Sometimes, when you're deep in thought trying to explain a subtle point, you subconsciously drift into a faint British accent. To your students, I'm sure, it only enhanced your air as an academic. When you did this with me and your colleagues, it brought chuckles and a ribbing…all in good fun. This might not play so well in your new profession."

"You're right, especially if I do this while answering a difficult sports question proposed to me in conversation at a bar. That might cause trouble of some sort."

"Well, we've got to train you," said George. "You'll have to learn how to talk like an out-of-town blue-collar tourist. We'll go to that new sports bar in town and hang out. You can start getting the feel of how things work and sound at that type of place. Quite different from what you're accustomed to." He smiled. "You can observe how the people act, how they talk, and what they drink and eat. None of which you are too familiar with. When you think you're ready, you can go by yourself to the bar. Dressed like a tourist you can practice talking and mingling like 'Charlie' until it comes somewhat naturally to you. I would think Jack Townsend has a special place he goes to, and I bet that's where you'll most likely be able to get in a conversation with him."

"For me to fool him, sitting in a bar having a chat without him recognizing me, will be a feat of grand proportions."

"Before you leave, you'll look, dress, and talk like you're a blue-collar tourist wandering around, his first time in Charleston. We'll work up a background story for you. Henry, this is going to be fun!" With a laugh, he slapped him on the back. "And be thinking of a name you'd like to use as the tourist."

Henry had thought about who might help him navigate in Charleston, as he had only visited it infrequently. He mentioned to George that he had some repairing to do in his relationship with Emily; he hoped this would present a good opportunity for him to do this but didn't want to burden her with thinking she had to babysit him. George said he had thought of this and had talked with Britt Pedersen, filling her in on Henry's new "operation." She agreed to be his contact, show him around town, and generally look out for him.

A transplant from New England, Britt had come to Charleston to attend Ashley Hall, a private girls' school, where she first met Martha. After graduating, they both attended Charleston College majoring in English. George had worked with Britt on various theater productions for almost twenty years, and although she had been Martha's best friend, Henry had only seen her occasionally over the years since first meeting her in college. George told him she was intelligent, level-headed, and knew she would be perfect to be his on-site mentor and confidant. Henry was relieved to hear that someone like Britt had agreed to help.

———

Six months after he had begun his alteration, Henry walked through campus as Charlie Andrews, the tourist. His appearance had completely changed. Nobody recognized him. He even had short conversations with students and a few of the professors. All of them thought he was from out of town, maybe Ohio.

"I'm just visitin' to see what this here place looks like." This, he smiled at.

He felt comfortable being "Charlie." *I'm ready.*

If he was going to leave, he would need to pack for a trip that had no timeline—a week? A month? Three months? Longer? He'd never packed by himself for any trip that he could remember. He found suitcases in the attic, brought them down to their bedroom, and stuffed them with his new clothes, his notes on various sports, and special reminders on the new character he would become. As he sat on the bed, it occurred to him that these were all new things he'd be living with. This led him to consider the special belongings and items he could *not* take with him. Things that had comforted him over the years that would not be beside him or within reach when he needed them: his dog, Falstaff, his study, his library of books, his dahlia garden, his MG, his small sailboat—all of his things. He would feel naked without them. And now, he was about to leave them all behind. He choked up at the thought.

Henry cleared his head, feeling that it was time to alert Emily of what he was about to do. He decided to make his call from the kitchen and sat in the hardback chair at the kitchen table. Not having spoken to her since the day of the funeral, he felt both pride and trepidation as he heard her phone ring.

"Hello?" she said.

"Hi, Emily, it's me. I'm calling with a bit of news. I've taken your advice to do something that I think would make your mom proud," he said, feeling his self-esteem rise just a notch.

"It's not returning to teach another semester at the college, is it?"

He could hear the cynicism in her voice and was not surprised. Still, it deflated him for a moment. He gathered a strong voice, replying, "I'm coming to Charleston to find the person who killed her. I believe it was not an accident."

Silence came over the phone and Henry looked to see if they were still connected.

"Have you gone mad?" she finally asked.

A good question, he thought. He had asked himself the same thing.

"I think not, Emily. After sitting for weeks in my study, grieving over her death and feeling all was lost, I came close to ending everything. Then

I realized that to save myself, I must go to Charleston and at least try and find the person who killed her. It's something I must do."

"Dad, that's a very noble thought, but I don't think you're equipped to undertake such a thing. It's not in your nature, not to mention your complete ignorance of how one would go about trying to solve a murder… if there was one."

It flashed through his mind that she had called him Dad, and not Henry. His heart swelled.

"You have a point, Emily, but I have worked hard to prepare myself as best I can and feel I must proceed. That, or return to my study and risk the inevitable consequence." He slumped in his chair at the thought of bailing out at this point and having to return to his study, defeated.

"I will be here to help in any way I can," she said, her voice growing quiet. "I admire you, Dad, but it scares the shit out of me."

"My sentiments exactly," he admitted, "but I'll see you in a few days."

Taking a seat, he let his eyes wander around the kitchen and the table his family would gather around. Although more of an observer, he enjoyed watching Martha, Emily, and Phillip interact. Now, half of his family was gone, and in some ways, he felt responsible for the death of both Phillip and Martha. Also, he had drifted lately into almost an estrangement with Emily with his inattentive behavior toward her for reasons he couldn't explain. And not far from his mind, there was Carl Muncie, the boy he had beaten so badly in high school. That dark cloud had never gone away.

Henry seemed unable to shake this reappearing cycle of incidents that brought grief and guilt to him throughout his life. Now, he wondered if he could he expect anything but more of the same in his future. Away from his cocoon here at the college, he feared what might happen in Charleston and how his story might end.

———

Hesitating once again, Henry stood on the front stoop of his house with George, suitcases loaded in his rented black Camry—waiting for the starting gun. He had completed his preparation and transformation but couldn't seem to get to the car and start the engine. It was like he had taken a course in sky diving and was now at three thousand feet standing in the open doorway of the plane and having to take that first step.

He looked at George. "I feel more like Don Quixote off to chase wind-mills than Hamlet," he said.

"I think you're a little of each of them, with each of their best qualities."

"They both died at the end of their stories. I may well have an appoint-ment in Samarra."

"You'll be just fine. Now get on your horse and ride into town."

The phone buzzed in Henry's pocket. He pulled it out, saw who it was, and answered. "Hi, Emily, how are you doing?" He listened a moment. "Stay inside until I get there. I'm

getting in the car right now. And, Emily, don't tell anyone I'm coming."

He took a deep breath and turned to George. His voice shaking, he whis-pered, "Jack Townsend is having Emily followed. That son of a bitch better not get near her." Jumping off the stoop, he ran to his car and sped away.

# CHAPTER 10

In his haste to get to Charleston, Henry drove five miles an hour over the speed limit on the interstate. In his mind, he was living on the edge. Now, alone in the car, the initial spirit for this adventure of his had dissipated with Emily's call. Everything was suddenly very real. On the road to Charleston, he realized that he may be "new" on the outside, but he still felt like the "old" Henry on the inside. Martha would be shaking her head in dismay if she knew what he had signed up for, even though it might appear to be a gallant gesture. Emily had called and pushed him off the starting line. There's no turning back now.

---

It was late in the afternoon when he parked on the street lined with palmetto palms less than a block from Emily's apartment. She had found the spacious unit some years before on the ground floor of a two-story colonial house built in the early nineteenth century. Two units on the second floor were rented to graduate medical students. Stepping out of his car, the late afternoon heat enveloped him. He stopped for a second to regain his equilibrium. Still unsure of their relationship since Martha's death, he hoped his arrival would show that he had committed to finding out what happened to his wife, her mother. Dressed in a white polo shirt, seersucker pants, and loafers, he could pass for a local real estate agent, attorney, or businessman. He looked appropriate for the neighborhood. As he neared the house and the actuality of starting, the bounce in his step after arriving had disappeared.

Set behind a small courtyard surrounded by a black wrought iron fence, the entrance was filled with azaleas, jasmine, and crepe myrtle trees covered with bright pink flowers. He stopped at her polished wood front door. The heat dropped over him like a wet blanket. He closed his eyes and tried to breathe slowly, evenly. He reached toward the doorbell, but stopped, letting his hand drop. Closing his eyes for a moment, he inhaled the sweet scent of jasmine. Opening his eyes, he forced a smile and rang the bell.

Emily opened the door.

She was dressed casually in jeans and a white men's shirt, the sleeves rolled to the elbows, the tails hanging out. She looked at him with an inquisitive face. Again, Henry was stunned by how much she looked like Martha in her early thirties.

"Yes, may I help you?" she asked.

"It's me, Emily. Henry. Dad."

She stepped back, her hand to her mouth, her eyes wide.

"Is that you? You scared me for a moment." She stepped out and hugged him as tears welled in his eyes. "Come in, come in. What happened? What did you do?" She backed up further to look, her green eyes curious but excited.

Henry stepped in, smiling.

"Been working out and George had me spruced up a bit. We thought a new look would help boost my confidence in taking on this endeavor. What do you think?" The loss of forty-five pounds was most striking and now with his hair trimmed close and beard shaved off, contact lenses with blue lens, and new clothes, he was the new Henry on the outside.

"It's quite something. I must say, you look great." She stared with an unbelieving look. "Nobody will recognize you."

"That, in itself, will help me navigate in this unknown world I've signed up for." He felt relieved at her welcoming, proud that he had made it this far.

"It's been a long drive today at excess speeds that scared me, but before we start into Jack Townsend, would you happen to have a beer in the fridge?"

Laughing, she leaned on the kitchen counter and looked back at him. "I've never heard you, or known of you, to ask for a beer in my life. Have you gone blue-collar on us? You watch NASCAR now?"

"I thought I looked more like an art dealer today, in town to select a few paintings for a collector." He slipped into a country drawl. "But if you'd rather kick around racin', and this week's race in Darlington, I'd be happy to oblige."

"You almost scare me!" she said, laughing again. "Go sit down and I'll get us something to drink."

"I know a Bud Light from craft beer these days, but a small glass of cabernet would be preferable, if you have some. I've been limited to one glass a day for the last two months by Nurse Ratchet down at the gym, so this will be a celebration of sorts for officially making it to Charleston."

He sat on a sofa and looked around at her home. He was ashamed to admit it was the first time in years. The eclectic mix of antique and modern furniture, burnished wood floors, a scattering of oriental rugs, and abstract and English prints and paintings on the walls. Henry thought how it mirrored how Emily had evolved and who she had become since her first years in college. She's now her own woman.

Emily returned with a glass of wine and a beer for herself. She sat across from him and leaned over, her elbows on her knees.

"I believe Jack Townsend's son is stalking me. I've had friends who work in restaurants tell me that he's asked who I was. He used a credit card with the name Jack Townsend on it. His name is Patrick, and I've seen him numerous times in restaurants and caught him staring at me. He's a skinny kid, kinda cute, must be in his twenties, I'd guess." She took a sip of her beer while pulling a couple strays of her auburn hair back over her ear. "I saw him again the other night when my friend Byron and I were out. As we were leaving, I stopped in front of him and asked why he was following me.

He denied it, of course, but Byron, being the jealous type, threatened him on the spot and was about to hit him when I grabbed his arm and talked him down. Funny, but this Patrick guy didn't blink an eye at Byron's threat. He just sat there and smiled—and Byron's a pretty big guy."

Hearing this, Henry's breathing became rapid and shallow. He was unsure of what to say, as he was overcome by the thought of his daughter and her date almost getting in a fight at a restaurant. My God, he thought, what if this Byron guy had punched this skinny youngster? He would be under arrest for battery and Emily might be charged as an accessory. Henry wasn't sure how these things worked in Charleston, but the possible consequences had him reeling.

"Do you have any clue, any intuition, as to why this Patrick is following you?"

"Not really. If Jack Townsend had something to do with Mom's death, why would he have his son following me? I can't seem to come up with a motive for him to do this." She took a long sip of her beer before slowly placing it down on the table. She looked up. "Should we just go find Jack and ask him just what the fuck is he doing?"

The thought sounded reasonable to Henry, but it also scared the hell out of him.

"I'm not sure that's a such a good idea right now." He thought a moment. "Let me see what I can find out on my own. Maybe I can spot something that could get the police involved somehow without us getting in a showdown with him alone." Henry had been on the job for less than an hour and already doubted himself for being able to cope with a simple situation like this.

"Well, Patrick hasn't done anything against the law," said Emily. "It could just be coincidences that I see him in restaurants regularly. He wouldn't know where I was going to go eat, anyway. Unless he follows me somehow, which would be hard to do. It's just unnerving having him around under the circumstances."

"Let's not tell anyone else that I'm in town. I'm still in North Carolina, as far as you know. Still a plump, stuffy professor. Britt will be the only other one who knows. Which reminds me, I need to see her this afternoon to find out where my apartment is located." Frowning, he looked off for a moment. "I have an idea. Let me know when and where you're going out to dinner, and I'll see if I can follow the guy who's following you. You figure out a way to signal me who he is." He shook his head. "Can you believe your father is talking like this? I'm about to step over a line and I'm not sure I'm capable of getting over it."

———

It was late in the afternoon when Henry found Britt's condo. Down a narrow cobblestone street not far from the college, it sat in a row of small two-hundred-year-old ivy-covered brick houses standing in permanent shade from palmetto palms and live oak trees. He knocked on the door, and when Britt opened it, he received similar looks of surprise and words of astonishment that Emily had given.

Henry had forgotten how tall she was. She stared him in the eye in her bare feet. Slim with long blond hair and blue eyes, Henry had always thought she had an athletic Nordic look about her. She and Martha had been close friends for over thirty-five years. They had first met at Ashley Hall Girls' School and continued on to Charleston College, both majoring in English lit. After college, Martha had married Henry, and they moved to Southern College to begin their careers. Britt moved back to her home in upstate New York, returning to Charleston College ten years later to join the English department. Her and Martha's friendship had blossomed once again.

Britt led him into her living room, tastefully furnished in modern furniture and pale woods. She had never married and had devoted her life to the drama department at the college. Her major interest was in English literature, which was Martha's specialty, so there was an ongoing bond between them—both personally and professionally. Many times, Henry felt like the odd man out, overpowered when he was present with them after everyone had had a few drinks and they took off debating the merits of various authors, playwrights, productions, and such. But he loved watching and listening to them, as well as the exuberance they showed in making their points.

"What a surprise you are, Henry. I could never have imagined you looking like this and taking on a task so out of character."

Britt brought wine for them both and sat down across from him.

"Well, welcome to Charleston. Cheers to a successful journey." They tipped their glasses to one other. "George called me and asked if I would help you navigate the city and its ways. I must admit, I was about to turn it down. I felt I could not hold up emotionally to the thought of talking over matters concerning Martha for however long you needed me. But George convinced me, and I'm grateful to you for what you're undertaking. I'll help all I can. We all need to know what happened."

She stood and turned away. "I hope you don't mind if I have a cigarette," she said, walking to the kitchen counter. "I'd stopped some years ago, but since…" She lit the cigarette and leaned on the counter. Straightening up, she wiped tears from her eyes and turned to him. "I still can't believe what happened."

Out of words, Henry dropped his head.

"I knew Martha as well as most, and I know how strong she could be. Once she made up her mind to do something, she usually got her way… especially with you." She put out her cigarette, walked back to her chair, and slumped down. "I'm so sorry."

Henry sat forward and set his wine down on the table.

"Thank you, Britt. No one knows what really happened. That's why I'm here."

He walked to the window that looked out onto a small courtyard, lush with plants. Turning, he said, "I've thought this through and I'm certain that Jack Townsend somehow had a hand in Martha's death. And I'll find out what it was, and then I'll do what I believe should be done."

"I admire what you've set out to do. And to get started, I've found a small condo for you to rent less than a block from where he lives. George told me that's what you wanted."

"It is. And thanks for volunteering to help guide me through this. I'll buy you dinner if you know a restaurant where we can get a decent meal." He grinned at his understatement.

"Oh, I know a restaurant near your place that you might like. Low-key, good food and drink, and a favorite of the locals."

Britt showed him his small apartment above a flower shop. A nicely furnished one-bedroom with original heart pine flooring, an open kitchen and sitting area, and large divided-light windows facing onto Meeting Street. Close by, around the corner, they walked to a cozy Mediterranean restaurant on King Street and took the small wood table at the corner window. The dinner crowd was sparse at this early hour, but the bar was busy with the young after-work crowd. Britt ordered a pinot grigio, Henry a cabernet along with appetizers.

"I've put together a list of contacts here in town," began Britt, sliding a few sheets of paper across the table, "of everyone I know who might have information that might help you, along with their addresses—everyone from the mayor on down to the head of parks and recreation who have authority over the public boat ramps. The names with asterisks are those I know personally, which you may mention if you talk to them."

"Thanks, this'll be a big help," he said, looking over the names. He hesitated a moment before he asked a question, knowing it went to the heart of his being there. "Britt, you knew Martha as well, or maybe better than anyone. What do you think happened that night?"

She took a sip of her wine.

"I've thought about this a lot," she said, gazing out the window a moment. "In the end, all I can come up with is that she drove in there by mistake. That was as bad a storm as I've seen in some time. But how do you drive down a ramp and into water so deep that you can't get out, and drown? Martha didn't make mistakes—not many, anyway. And as far as someone driving her down there—first of all, who would have wanted to kill her? She had no enemies that I know of. Besides, how would a person actually do such a thing? None of it makes sense to me."

"To me, either. But the only lead I have is Jack Townsend. I found out he was a fighter pilot in the navy and was released early because of insubordination, brawling in bars, and a quick temper that continually brought trouble. And he showed it that afternoon in the restaurant in front of Martha."

"As you probably know, I dated him twice about a year ago," she said casually, "and—"

"You what?" Henry broke in. "How did that happen?"

"—met him at an art exhibit at the college. He couldn't identify a Picasso from a Rembrandt, but he was a fun date. I told Martha about it later and we both laughed over it; she was getting cards and flowers from him on and off over the years. He's a little younger than Martha and we thought it was like he had a high school crush on her. Anyway, I didn't see any future with him."

Henry was stunned.

"I don't believe it. Martha never mentioned your dating Townsend to me." He looked puzzled.

"She probably just forgot. We only talked about it for a few minutes. Jack Townsend was not someone you spent much time thinking about." She sipped her wine. "But I can't see him doing something like this."

"Did he know you were still good friends with Martha? He'd seen you together back in college. Did he ask about her? Anything at all?"

"No, Martha was never mentioned. The conversations were generally limited to Jack talking about himself or his latest exploits. He's really quite proud of himself."

"Did he ever lose his temper in front of you, or make you feel threatened in any way?"

"No, not at all."

"Was Martha distracted by anything going on in her life that she may have confided in you that she was upset about?"

"She had been upset for months at Emily for going to law school instead of continuing on her English lit track. She thought it better to expose young people to great historical literature and all that it could teach them about life. She considered the law a cutthroat profession with few morals."

"That's strange. She never mentioned her objections to Emily's change of direction. But that was some months ago. I wouldn't think she'd still be dwelling on it."

"Well, there's nothing else that I can put my finger on that might have distracted her. I'm upset that my best friend died, but I'm also *mad* at her for driving into the water. Such a senseless mistake." Shaking her head, she stared off a moment. Turning back, she said in a low voice, "Shall we go ahead and order?"

"Of course," said Henry. Suddenly, it came to him that Britt might be able to verify something that had unsettled him since the funeral.

"By the way, do you know what kind of car Jack drives?"

"A red Corvette convertible. Why?"

# CHAPTER 11

Awakening in a strange bed, with early morning sun beaming through tall windows, Henry sat up, disoriented. It took a moment for him to remember he was in Charleston in a rented apartment over a retail store on Meeting Street—and he was alone. The reality of it all hit him like a slap in the face. He felt as if any courage he had mustered up along the way was escaping from his heart and slowly draining from his bones. He lay back and looked out the window, not sure he was capable of walking out on the street and begin being the person he wasn't. He swore to himself for hesitating and got up. Britt had stocked his refrigerator with a small assortment of food and drink, so he was able to feed himself, at least in the mornings. With a bowl of yogurt and blueberries, along with a cup of coffee, he sat at the small table by the window that looked out onto the street. He wished he could open the window and feel the cool mountain breeze he was accustomed to in the summer mornings at home. But he knew the air outside was already hot and thick with humidity. He smiled, glad he was now a much slimmer version of himself, more capable of coping with the heat than the old version.

Last night, he had promised himself that today he would begin his investigation. The images of the nightmare no longer came upon him as often these days, but he realized he would be stepping back into those twenty-four hours that had turned his life upside down.

Today, he would be Henry Willis. He dressed casually and decided he would start at the parking garage. He entered the parking garage and began driving up the ramp to where he and Martha had parked on the third level. At the second level, he stopped for a moment, closed his eyes, and took a deep breath. Sitting up straight, eyes wide, he continued up to the third level and parked. He leaned against the car, reliving that night when he had searched for her and tried to imagine what had happened here. His chest tightened as he looked around the ugly concrete edifice and imagined what secrets it carried. Chilled from the thoughts, he forced himself to move and walk to the elevator.

Out on the street, the blazing sun felt good on his back after his stay in the garage. His short walk to the Chez Toulouse was bright and dry, with the sidewalks filled with people.

At the restaurant, he asked for Francois, giving a server his name. He looked at their table by the window and could almost see her there, waiting for him. She would not be upset with him this time, nor would he be nervously thinking of an explanation to offer. He wished with all his heart he could begin a replay of that evening right now. And when it was time to leave, we would leave together.

Francois arrived. It took a minute for Henry to convince him it was him, whereupon Francois gave him a big hug and expressed his condolences for the loss of Martha.

"Please stay and have lunch with us, Mr. Willis—on the house, of course."

"Thank you, but I can't today," said Henry. "I do have a question for you, though. Have you seen the man again who was at our table that evening?"

"No, but I explained to the police how the man jumped up from your table, spilling wine, and almost knocked me down in his haste to leave." Francois became animated, as his story gained momentum and his hands flew up in the air. "And he just threw open the front door and walked out with rain blowing into our beautiful restaurant. Mon Dieu, I was mad!"

"Did anyone notice which way he went when he left?" Henry hoped he would say to the right, the direction Martha took to the garage, to confirm his suspicions.

"Oh, yes! Peter, our head waiter, ran to close the door and looked outside for a moment. The man was standing down the sidewalk, on the corner." He pointed to his right. "Just standing there in the rain, with no umbrella." He shook his head.

Jack Townsend was standing in the path Martha would take to the garage, thought Henry.

"Would you mind if I sat at our table for a moment?" asked Henry. "Maybe a cup of coffee would be nice."

"But of course. Take your time. I'll send you coffee and a pastry."

Francois escorted him to their table where he sat on Martha's side, facing the door.

Henry had a thought. He motioned to Francois, saying, "A question just came to mind that you may be able to help me with. How were Martha and I able to get our favorite table by the window that night during the early dinner rush without a reservation?"

"Let me check our reservation book. I'll be right back."

He walked over to his stand for a minute and immediately returned.

"Ah, just as I thought. It was Britt Pederson. Martha always had her make a reservation for your table for at least one night whenever you were planning on coming to town. Martha would make a guess as to what night it would be and alert Britt, and it usually worked out. It was a habit of hers."

Henry nodded.

"It makes sense. It's something Martha would do. We always made a point of eating here when we were in town, so it worked out for everybody. Thanks for all you've done for us over the years, Francois."

Henry had not planned on returning to their table for fear of facing the memories of where the nightmare began, but he had steeled himself for what he knew he would have to face. Sitting at their table, he could not help but think of that evening. He found his hand shaking and had to grab the coffee cup with both hands. He had to change the direction of his thoughts to get on with the business of the day.

Henry reached in his pocket and brought out his small map of downtown Charleston. He asked to borrow a pencil before marking the location of the restaurant, garage, and boat ramp. He then marked the obvious route back to the front of the restaurant from the garage, the route Martha would have taken. It involved making a right turn out of the garage onto Third Avenue, going to the end of the block to the stoplight at Church Street, with the boat ramp entrance directly across from the intersection. Then, take a right on Church, take the next two rights and you're back on King, a block from the restaurant. How easy can it be…four rights and here you are.

Henry thought that Jack probably figured he had ruined our dinner and it wouldn't be long before we would come out. When Martha left alone for the garage, it was a stroke of luck for him. Following her up the ramps to the car and approaching her alone at the car would be much easier. Henry wondered if they had talked first, or had he just slipped up on her from behind. How he got her to the ramp and in the water without a trace that anyone else had been in the car was a more difficult question. That question had to be answered here in Charleston.

Henry finished his coffee, thanked Francois, and walked to the garage and his car. He took a right out of the garage and drove one block to the light and stopped. The boat ramp lay straight ahead. On green, he drove forward slowly toward the entrance and stopped in front of the metal cross-arms, installed shortly after Martha's death, blocking the entrance into the ramp area. He slid his credit card in the meter beside the car for the five-dollar toll, and the gate swung open. No boats were launching or returning at midday. The area was still. His hands tightened on the steering wheel as he inched forward to where the ramp began its descent into the river and stopped. He stared at the tranquil river meandering downstream toward the harbor, imagining Martha strapped in their car—underwater—in that river for almost twelve hours. His initial grief at the thought of her sitting there slowly transformed to rage at the person he thought responsible for putting her there. The man who had waited for her in the rain.

Henry had read that most near-death accounts from persons dragged to safety while unconscious told of how they held their breath for as long as they could, but when they tried to take the next breath, they breathed only water before all went dark. Henry thought of the waterboarding torture which emulates drowning and the outcry that it was cruel and unusual torture. The thought of Martha experiencing this made him dizzy with anger.

He got out and stood beside the front of the car. The smell of salt water and marsh grass engulfed him as distant memories of him and Martha in college days playing on the beach rolled through his mind. Swallowing hard, he shook his head. He stared at the dark water, trying to visualize a car driving down the ramp and into the water. How far does it go before it stops? He had read that a person might have only sixty seconds to escape a sinking car by crawling through a window. The doors cannot be opened because of the water pressure against them. He wondered why Martha had been unable to unfasten her seat belt.

He heard a vehicle make a sharp stop behind him. He turned to see a patrol car with the driver's side door open, lights flashing. There was no siren. An officer got out and walked toward him. Henry stood and waited.

"You planning on going fishing in that Camry, sir?" said the young patrolman, with the hint of a smile.

"Uh, no sir," was all Henry could come up with.

"You might want to back away from the ramp a bit. Don't want you to accidentally drive or slide down into the water."

"Yes sir, I'll do that." He took a step back.

"You mind telling me what you're doing with your car at a boat ramp with no boat?"

"That's a fair question, officer." Henry debated on how to answer. "Do you remember a few months back when a lady was found sitting in her car, underwater, drowned, at the bottom of this ramp?"

The patrolman started a bit, a quizzical look on his face.

"I was on duty that morning and one of the first responders here. Why?"

"That woman—" Henry choked, struggling to finish the sentence. "That woman was my wife, Martha Willis." He slid his hands into his pockets and looked off for a moment.

The patrolman's look softened.

"I'm sorry for your loss, Mr. Willis. I must say I've never seen…" Stopping, he took a step back. "May I help you get safely away from the area?"

"Yes, you may." He looked at the name tag on the policeman's shirt. "Sergeant Mitchell, thank you for your service on that morning." Stepping forward, he shook the police officer's hand and got in his car.

He looked out again at the ramp and the flowing river and, with tears in his eyes, slammed his hands hard against the steering wheel. All of his sorrow had turned to fury at Jack Townsend.

Henry pulled out his wallet and retrieved the note with information about the location where their old car had been parked. He drove away from the boat ramp and headed for the North Charleston salvage yard to find the Buick that carried Martha to her death. He had not seen it since parking it that afternoon before their retirement party at the college. After the car was found in the river, he had not been able to bring himself to look at it. Now, he would go face it.

However, the closer he got to the salvage yard, the more his determination to see the car faded. By the time he entered the sprawling graveyard of abandoned, rusted vehicles, he hoped it wasn't there. But the man at the gate remembered it and gave him directions to find it. For some time, Henry puttered about the lot as if he'd lost interest in the whole endeavor. Almost by accident, he spotted the dark blue Buick. He parked close by, got out, leaned against his car, and stared at their old car. The sun beat down through the thick, still air and he found it hard to breathe. From the outside, it did not look like a murder weapon. Yet, he hesitated to approach it, afraid to discover what might still be inside. He gathered himself, walked to the car, and after some effort, managed to get the driver's side door open. He looked in and gasped, having to turn away for a moment. Pieces of cut seat belt lay on the seat where the EMTs had cut Martha loose to extract her from the vehicle.

Clenching his teeth, Henry forced himself to sit down. He tried to piece it together. Jack would have moved her from the garage to the river and left her underwater buckled in her seat with no sign of him ever being there. Jack would have followed her to the car, called to her, apologized for his behavior at the restaurant, and asked if they could sit and talk for just a minute. Martha would have agreed, and Jack would have sat down in the passenger seat. He would have had to knock her out somehow, without a trace, slide her over on the bench seat to the passenger side, drive her to the boat ramp, switch seats again, buckle her up, and from the passenger side, drive her into the water and climb out through the window as the water rose. He closed his eyes and imagined Martha sitting there, unable to escape, as the water quickly rose. Just before the water reached his mouth, he took a deep breath and held it. It covered his head, and he couldn't hold it any longer. He inhaled greedily for air and found it. But Martha had found only salt water. Shuddering, he slumped in the seat, exhausted as tears swelled in his eyes. He didn't remember how long he sat there, unmoving.

Finally, he looked around and saw nothing out of place. He got out and walked around the car opening all the doors and searching inside—for what, he didn't know. He looked under the front seat and poked around. Nothing. The trunk was empty. He had discovered nothing but more grief.

His last stop of the day was the one he dreaded most. At the police station, he met with Sgt. Winslow, who led the investigation into Martha's drowning. Her file was pulled, and Henry read through the transcript of events, beginning with his call from the garage reporting that she was missing, to the discovery of her body at the Third Avenue boat ramp the following morning. A summary of the investigation into her death included interviews with various people who knew her or were in attendance at the retirement ceremony and the employees at Chez Toulouse. He read all of the interrogations. Jack Townsend did not have an alibi that could be verified, nor did ten other people, including Emily, Britt, George, and five other people whose names Henry recognized. Security cameras in the parking garage did not show her car leaving, although power had been lost for forty-five minutes, which fit into the time frame of Martha entering the garage. All power around the intersection of Third Avenue and Church Street, including the stoplight at the intersection with the entrance to the boat ramp, was also lost during that same timeframe. At the boat ramp, the security arm was not yet installed. The wooden barricades had been blown and pushed by the storm waters off to the side. The yellow warning tape across the entrance had been blown into nearby bushes and trees. Overhead lights for the area had not yet been installed. The cell phone he found crushed in the parking garage that night was identified as Martha's, but the police were unable to extract information from the phone.

The most difficult task was looking through the file of photos. He studied the photos taken of the interior of the car, both before and after Martha had been extracted. He was looking for anything that didn't look normal. The front seat didn't appear normal to most people, as it was a retro bench seat, without a console dividing the two front seats. Martha always carried her Yorkshire terrier, Fluffy, beside her, with his own seat restraint. Their 2011 was the last model that Buick made with a bench seat option. It was either that or a pickup truck.

Henry sat there, wondering if it might be possible: In a driving rainstorm at night, with no streetlights or stoplights working and no gate in place, could a person not paying attention mistakenly enter from Third Avenue and drive straight down the ramp before they realized what was happening?

He scanned the coroner's report and that of the forensics lab, most of it generally undecipherable to him, other than it was deemed to be an accidental drowning. The name at the bottom of the toxicology report caught his eye, making his whole body twitch involuntarily. He placed the report back on the table.

"No, it couldn't be," he murmured to himself, leaning over and looking again at the name and signature. This is not possible.

# CHAPTER 12

His head swimming, Henry hurried to his apartment and opened his laptop. He pulled up the city government website, which confirmed that Carl Muncie, from Cool Springs, North Carolina, was the head of the toxicology department. A flood of shame swept over Henry again as he remembered that day; it surfaced in a clarity he had not experienced in decades. He stared off, seeing that rainy afternoon in high school as if it were yesterday.

———

*As he passed the last two runners ahead of him, he could see the finish line through the pouring rain. Only a few more seconds to hold on. His heart raced as he splashed through the puddles of water on the muddy field. He was in grasp of the county cross-country championship. He would make his father proud in a way that had always eluded Henry. He would be excelling in a sport, even though it wasn't football. In his father's eyes, his accolades in academics had never quite measured up to playing high school football in their small town. His father had never said so in as many words, but Henry knew. He had begged his father to come and watch this race and was overjoyed to spot him standing near the finish line under a black umbrella. Henry needed this win, at this moment, more than anything in his life.*

*Suddenly, he tripped and fell into the muddy water. He looked over his shoulder and saw Carl Muncie lying on the ground right behind him, as Will Musgrove came running by. Just like that, it was all over. He looked up and saw his father turn and walk away.*

*Henry whirled around, saw Carl on his knees about to get up. Thinking Carl had tripped him on purpose, Henry sprang at him, knocked him down, and began pummeling him with his fists, shouting obscenities. It took three other runners to finally pull him off. He heard his coach yelling for help to take Carl to the emergency room. Sitting in the water, Henry stared blankly ahead, not believing what had just happened. His father appeared and squatted down in front of him. The man just glared, showing nothing but contempt. Tears began to well in Henry's eyes.*

———

Although he had tried for months afterward, Henry had not seen Carl or spoken to him since that day. Carl and his family had shut the door on Henry Willis as had, to a lesser extent, his own family. He had been charged with simple assault, a misdemeanor, put on probation, and directed to enter anger management counseling. That one day and its consequences had tempered his personality for life.

Henry knew that he must go and talk to Carl Muncie. He'd been carrying this albatross around his neck for more than thirty years and now, for the first time, he had an opportunity to see if it might be possible to make amends. He learned Carl was still a runner, competing in the annual Cooper River Bridge Run and various 5K events around the area. He made an appointment to see Carl, so as not to surprise him unannounced.

The following day, before his appointment, Henry paced the floor in his apartment, practicing over and over what he would say to Carl. He knew this would be one of the most difficult tasks of his life—other than identifying Martha at the morgue.

He stopped at the front desk of the toxicology department and was directed to Dr. Muncie's office. Walking down the hall toward the office, he tried to slow his breathing. He could hear his heartbeat in his ears. Sweating, he pulled a wad of Kleenex from his pocket, wiped his face, and plodded on. Coming to a glass door with *Carl Muncie, Director of Toxicology* printed on it, he leaned against the wall for a moment before he looked in and saw Carl for the first time in forty years, studying papers on his desk. He was thin, like most dedicated runners, with receding hair and thick glasses. He looked like one would expect a forensic lab scientist to look. Stepping back for a moment, Henry took a deep breath before knocking on the door. He opened it enough to stick his head in.

"Mr. Muncie," he said, "it's Henry Willis. May I come in?"

Carl looked up, staring a moment.

"Hello, Henry. Come in. It's been a while." He nodded toward a seat in front of his desk.

"Too long, I'm afraid," said Henry as he sat. "Thank you for seeing me, I didn't know if you would after all this time." He held his breath, trying to slow his racing heart.

"I was sorry to see your wife had died…especially under such strange circumstances."

"That's why I'm in Charleston, trying to find out what really happened. She was not the type of person to drive down a boat ramp and into the water by mistake…even in the weather conditions of that night." He pushed on with what he had come to say. "Just, as I later found out, you were not the type of person to run into another runner by mistake, even if it was muddy and raining. You were bumped into me by Will Musgrove, who went on to win the race. And I thought you tripped me by your carelessness. I know this is forty years too late, but I am sorry I did such a thing to you. I have no excuse, and I have not been the same person since that day."

Taking off his glasses, Carl lay them on his desk.

"And I have not been the same person since that day." He stared long at Henry. "I did find out later that you had sent letters to me and that my parents returned to you unopened. Later, I wished they had saved them for me. But at the time I understood why they didn't. I wouldn't have read them anyway."

"I have lived with the guilt of what I did and I'm ashamed that I never had the courage to try and find you. It took the death of my wife to bring me to Charleston and, by chance, to see your name on her paperwork. It gave me the opportunity to try and talk to you. Thank you for giving that to me. I needed to do this." He paused. "I consider it the one good thing that has come from her death." Although his mouth was dry, he was relieved to have been able to get the words out.

"Tell me, Henry, what can I help you with?" he asked as he put on his glasses.

Clearing his throat, he took a breath before continuing on.

"Martha left the restaurant to get the car in the garage a block and a half away around seven-thirty that night. About thirty or forty minutes later, I discovered her car missing from the garage. The drive from the garage directly to the boat ramp is just over a block away. Assuming she drove, or was driven, directly to the ramp, she would have been in the water around 7:45 p.m. or eight o'clock. I have learned that in such a situation, a person has about one minute to get out of the car before being completely submerged underwater, with death following shortly afterward. Does this sound about right to you?"

"That's more or less how it could play out."

"Did you estimate a time of death for her?" asked Henry.

Carl pulled a file from his file drawer. "Time of death was estimated at between 8:00 and 9:00 p.m."

"The autopsy said she died of drowning. Would you please explain to me exactly what happens when you drown?" Henry felt uncomfortable with the short questions and answers, the back and forth. It felt as if he were interrogating someone on the witness stand.

"A small amount of water enters the trachea and causes a muscle spasm that seals the airway and prevents further passage of water. This is followed by a loss of consciousness due to hypoxia. In most cases, the trachea relaxes sometime after unconsciousness and water can then enter the lungs, which is called wet drowning. Your wife had water in her lungs, which confirms she was alive when she drowned."

On hearing this, Henry felt faint; his body swayed, his eyes blinking. He managed to shake his head. A moment later, he recovered his mental balance. "Sorry," he mumbled.

"It's not uncommon for a person…" He paused. "Upon hearing the details of how a loved one has died to identify with the victim, almost feeling what that person must have felt, and reacting as you did." In a quiet voice, Carl added, "There's no shame in that."

His eyes down, Henry nodded weakly. He looked up.

"Can you tell me how much pain is experienced with drowning?"

"In her case, I believe it would have happened quite quickly with little pain."

"For that, I'm glad. The police told me there were no illegal drugs or controlled substances in her system?"

"That's correct."

"And no signs of a struggle or foul play?"

"None."

"She was in a good mood when she left the restaurant. I just find it hard to believe she just drove down the ramp and into the water, where she drowned. Sitting there." He thought for a moment. "Could she have had a heart attack from the shock of driving into the water like that?"

"Unlikely."

"To be candid, I believe someone killed her," Henry explained. "That's the reason I'm here in Charleston. To find that person. In trying to recreate what could have happened, I believe a person would have had to knock her out for about ten or fifteen minutes, switch seats with her and drive to the boat ramp, put her back in the driver's seat, buckle her up, and drive the car into the water and with the windows down, climb out of the passenger side window as the car filled with water. Since there were no signs of a struggle or bruising from a blow to the head, was there a drug that she could have been given to knock her out that would not have raised any red flags?"

"None that I discovered."

"Then, all the evidence points to a simple accident?" said Henry.

"That's our conclusion."

Henry sat in silence. There was nothing more to say. He stood.

"Thank you for seeing me." He was about to extend his hand but decided it might be presumptuous to do so. Carl nodded slightly and Henry walked out, feeling little better than when he entered.

# CHAPTER 13

enry decided it was time for him to hit the streets. He needed to set aside Henry and find out if he had it in him to become "Charlie," to dress and talk like "Charlie" and be believable. He would visit the Coffee Bar across the street from where Jack lived, get breakfast, and talk to Sally. *This will be my first real test.* He figured that to make his test more meaningful, he would ask her about apartment rentals in the area, as he had on his first trip to Charleston, and see if that triggered her memory.

Dressed in a cotton shirt, Bermuda shorts, white sneakers and socks, a baseball hat, and sunglasses, he looked like one of the thousands of summer tourists in the city. He walked into the café, filled with college students, businessmen, and a scattering of older retirees, and found a small table at the right wall and took a seat.

Within a minute, Sally walked up and asked if he'd like to start with coffee, showing no sign that she recognized him. As she poured the coffee, Henry looked at the menu and was about to order a yogurt parfait when he caught himself.

"I'll just have your egg, bacon, and cheese scramble please." Taking a breath, he looked up at her and started in. "I'm just visitin' and was wondrin' if there's any places to rent right around here. Haven't seen a realtor yet, but thought maybe you might have an idea."

"There are some units over the restaurants and retail stores," she said. "The only stand-alone units close by are across the street behind the big house. Realtors might be your best bet, or try Craigslist, which has everything on it."

"I'll just do that. Thanks."

As Sally walked away, he exhaled, thinking, Charlie's passed his first test.

Henry was starting into his scramble when he saw Jack Townsend walk in. His hands jerked and the eggs on his fork tumbled onto his plate. Dressed in a white shirt with epaulets on the shoulders, dark tie, and pants, Henry guessed he must have a flight today. Sally spoke to him at the door, pointing to a table toward the back. Jack ambled through the tables, saying hello to most everyone he passed. He knew the regulars and cast an eye at all the coeds along the way. He took a table across the room. Henry wasn't mentally prepared to possibly having to face Jack his first morning in town. He immediately regretted coming to the café.

He watched Jack out of the corner of his eye as Sally poured coffee for him and they chatted. Jack then glanced over at him for a second, turned back, and continued talking with Sally. Henry's heart was racing. He tried to continue eating, not daring to look in Jack's direction. He didn't know if Sally had recognized him and was retelling their encounter two months before or was simply asking if there were any vacancies across the street. He continued eating, his head down, when suddenly Jack was standing beside the table. His worst fears had arrived beside his table at eight o'clock in the morning.

"Excuse me," said Jack, "but Sally said you might be looking for a rental unit close by."

Henry looked up and tried to smile. He was unable to produce any words.

"I happen to live across the street," Jack continued, "and I could check if any of the other units are available, if you'd like. They're not handled by any agency, but I know the owner and could check."

Caught off guard, Henry brought his old acting course into play—when a line was forgotten, just start talking. "Sure, if you don't mind. Name's

Charlie Andrews. Stayin' with a friend for the moment. Maybe you could leave word with the waitress, and I'll stop back by in a few days?"

"Jack Townsend," he said, putting his hand out to shake.

Nodding, Henry shook his hand.

Jack hesitated a second. With one final look at Henry, he returned to his table.

Henry felt as if he'd just finished a session with Buster Lloyd and the heavy bag at the gym. Face-to-face real time with Jack wasn't like practicing back home with George at the college.

He kept an eye on Jack, but never caught him looking back at him. Sally kept him distracted, spending more time at his table than with any other customers. Finally, Jack paid his bill and walked out, without a single glance in his direction.

A sigh of relief passed silently over Henry. Sensing he may have stumbled across a key moment to follow Jack, he quickly retrieved his check, ordered a coffee and a doughnut to go, and left cash on the table with a generous tip for Sally.

Fortunately, he had parked his car in the street close by the café the night before. He was waiting in his Camry when Jack left the driveway in his red convertible about five minutes later. The luck he had stumbled on during his first morning in the city lifted his spirits. He had studied the map of Charleston and the various routes to the city airport from Jack's place; he was surprised when Jack started down Calhoun Street, a direction away from the airport. The heavy morning traffic and Jack speeding in his sports car made it difficult for Henry to keep him in sight without breaking various traffic laws along the way. He figured even if he was speeding to stay up with him, the police would pull over a red Corvette convertible before a black Camry. He followed him over various bridges and roads for twenty minutes to a small airport on Johns Island.

As he drove on, he saw Jack entering the terminal. He parked so he could watch both the terminal entrance and the tarmac. This was obviously not the airport for Air Carolinas, and he was curious what this might be about. Various private planes were parked along the far side. One small jet, which Henry surmised must be privately owned, was parked in front of the small terminal building. With its door open and gangway in place, Henry could see various people were coming and going inside as a fuel hose was disconnected from a wing. Henry chewed on the doughnut and drank his coffee, fascinated at the activities that preceded takeoff.

Ten minutes later, he saw Jack—walking out to the jet, now wearing a dark coat and pilot's cap—with someone who appeared to work at the airport.

A half hour later, a long black Mercedes stopped in front and a well-dressed gray-haired man exited from one side of the backseat as the chauffer opened the other door for an elegantly dressed woman. The man said something to the chauffer before he and the woman entered the terminal. They must be some of the passengers, Henry decided. There was someone in the cockpit and Henry assumed it must be Jack, as he had not left the plane.

A few minutes later, the well-dressed couple walked out on the tarmac to the plane. At the top of the stairs, they were greeted by a woman who appeared to be the flight attendant. The gangway retracted into the plane, the door closed, and the engines came to life.

Henry got out of his car and walked to the fence to better witness the takeoff. The jet taxied to the end of the runway, throttled up the engines, and shot down the runway, lifting its nose and jumping into the air. Henry had never watched a jet standing outside near the runway and heard the roar of the engines at takeoff. It took his breath away. As it gained altitude, it began a sweeping turn to the south. Transfixed, Henry watched until it disappeared from sight.

Back to business, he thought. Who are those two people and where are they going? And Jack is moonlighting as a private pilot on the side. Why? Does he need the extra money? And how does any of this fit in with Martha…if it does? He wondered how he might go about getting some answers to a few of these questions. Since he was dressed as a tourist, he had an idea.

He walked into the terminal, which was empty except for a man sweeping the floor. There was also a pleasant-looking young man with sandy hair standing behind a small counter, studying paperwork.

In his white sneakers, Henry approached the counter without a sound.

"Mornin'!" he said, louder than he needed.

The man jumped and looked up.

"Why, good morning. Didn't hear you coming. Can I help you?"

"Name's Charlie. I'm here on vacation, and I'm thinkin' about taking my family on vacation to the islands. Thought maybe a small airport like this might have better deals on gettin' a plane than the boys at the big airports."

"We do run a few charters out of here. My name's Sam. What do you have in mind?"

"I'd like to fly down to the Caribbean somewhere. There'd be four of us. Wife and me, and two kids. Maybe the Bahamas. Just so the sand's white and the water's clear. Maybe for a week or so. Not real sure yet."

Sam gave Henry a skeptical look.

"Well, if you nail down where and when you would like to go, I could run some numbers for you."

"You know, I was just thinkin'. I liked the look of that jet that just took off. Drove up just as they was loadin' her up. Were they on one of your charters and goin' to the islands?"

Sam shook his head. "No, that's a private jet. They were headed for Puerto Rico."

"Really! They got their own pilot and everything?"

"No, the pilot's from a commercial airline who's usually available for charter flights, with enough advance notice, that is. Mr. Middleton pays him directly in this case since he uses this same pilot every month."

"They got white sand and clear water in Porta Rica?"

"Sure do."

"Is that why these folks who just took off go there…in their private jet?"

"It's really none of our business why they go down there every month, but I think her family lives down there and she visits her mother for two or three days."

"Jeez, he must have a lot of money."

"I believe he's an attorney in Charleston, but he doesn't own the plane."

"Think maybe he'd let us ride along with him sometime to Porta Rica?"

Sam chuckled, apparently enjoying this spirited conversation.

"Kinda doubt it. His wife's father owns the plane, and I've only seen him take any other folks once. Must've been friends of his wife he took back in early spring, I think it was. Two ladies." He looked off wistfully for a second. "They were a pair. Nice looking, even though older than me. One with auburn hair, the other a blonde that looked Swedish and…" He stopped, as if realizing he was talking too much.

Henry flinched at the descriptions, which even though brief could fit hundreds of women. Given that the pilot was Jack Townsend tied it together in his mind for a moment. But could it be? Martha was in Charleston about two months before the retirement party for some conference or another, if he remembered correctly. Couldn't be. Too much of a coincidence.

Henry changed course. "Got a question. You gotta have a passport to go there?"

"Nope, it's a US territory."

"So, all we gotta do is show up with some money and get on."

Sam nodded, unable to hold back a grin. "Yup, that more or less sums it up, as best I've ever heard."

"That's nice and easy. Say, I gotta go. I'll stop back when I get it figured out."

"Been a pleasure," said Sam, rolling his eyes as Henry hurried off.

Henry left the airport and, within half a mile, found a small park. He pulled in under a large live oak tree and into the shade and took off his ball hat. He sat slumped in his car, exhausted from his performance. The AC struggled to lower the inside temperature down from the ninety-eight shown on the screen. Feeling both proud and surprised at what he had accomplished by acting like a tourist, Henry had to admit he enjoyed doing it. From Hamlet to Charlie. He reached into the glove compartment, took out a small spiral notepad and pen and began to make notes. He learned that Jack had a regular outside job once a month, receiving payment directly from a Mr. Middleton. What do they do in San Juan every month? Family, business, or maybe both? Who were the two ladies on the flight back in the spring? Is there a manifest I could get a look at? Was it Martha and Britt? No way. He would talk to Britt.

# CHAPTER 14

Buoyed by his initial success as "Charlie," Henry returned to town. He drove aimlessly around the narrow streets in the historic district, admiring the stately homes dating back to the eighteenth century. He made his way to the battery on the tip of the peninsula and found a parking space by the seawall. He walked up and planted his elbows on the railing, leaned forward, and watched four small sailboats racing out in the harbor, heeled over in the strong onshore breeze. He pictured himself sitting on the high side, the tiller in one hand as he responded to the wind shifts and its strength to keep the boat on its feet. Martha would think I'd gone mad to even think of doing such a thing out in the harbor. He smiled at the thought.

He realized he deserved a small reward for his first day of being Charlie, both in front of Jack and later at the airport. Britt had mentioned the cozy lounge at the Charleston Place Hotel, not far from the battery. He thought it would suit his mood to stop there and gather his thoughts.

Entering the hotel, he admired the white marble floors with two opposing circular stairs ascending to the second floor. Off to one side was a softly lit lounge. He took a seat in one of the overstuffed armchairs. Small seating areas were sprinkled about, with a grand piano in one corner and a small bar in the other. A young waitress stopped by and, even though dressed as Charlie, he needed comfort. So, he ordered a cup of hot tea and biscuits, then leaned back and exhaled.

Henry hadn't heard from Emily about an upcoming dinner with Byron, nor had Britt answered his phone call. He had forgotten that people had regular day jobs. Questions tumbled through his mind: Emily stalked by Patrick, plus Britt and Jack dating, and now a Mr. Middleton and the jet on which Jack served as his personal pilot. He also thought about Puerto Rico and the two ladies whose brief descriptions could possibly match Martha and Britt. What does all this mean? he wondered. He needed an organizational chart to get everybody lined up. He was exhausted after only a few days away from the comfort of his home.

The tea arrived. He sat back, enjoying delicate English biscuits as the soft music of Chopin drifted over the room, played by the young pianist on the piano. He closed his eyes and floated off to a country home in the English countryside, sitting out, sharing an aperitif with Martha. The place overlooked a lush, green lawn that sloped down to a garden of flowers surrounding a small pond, presently the home for a family of ducks and their chicks.

His reverie was interrupted by his teaspoon clinking on the side of his teacup. He started, opened his eyes, lost in where he was. Britt stood over him, smiling.

"Good afternoon. Is that you, Henry? Where were you just then?"

He hesitated. "I was in the English countryside with Martha."

"Take a deep breath and relax. I'm here to meet Byron, a friend from the college, for an afternoon drink. We just finished a rehearsal of *Macbeth* at the college." Looking at his teapot, she added, "Maybe it's time for a sip of something a little stronger?"

"Maybe you're right." He straightened up in his seat, massaging his temples for a moment.

"Have you been sightseeing?" she said as she sat down in an armchair. "I almost didn't recognize you in your Bermuda shorts and white tennis shoes. You're missing a camera around your neck, though." She studied him a moment. "You look puzzled about something."

"I was hoping to see you. I had quite an interesting morning as Charlie Andrews and wanted to get your take on what it all might means."

"Okay," she said, sitting down in an armchair. "So what did you get into all by yourself today, Charlie?"

Henry recounted how he saw Jack at the café, then followed him to a small airport where he watched him fly off in a small jet with a wealthy-looking couple.

"In the terminal, I acted like a curious tourist and Sam, the man behind the counter, told me the pilot flies them to Puerto Rico every month for a weekend. I asked whether he ever took any other passengers, and he said a couple months ago he took two ladies with them. Sam, who looked to be in his thirties, said they were attractive older ladies, one with auburn hair, the other a blond, Swedish-looking lady. Sam stopped when he realized he had said too much. I couldn't help but think of you and Martha, and Jack's connection. Am I crazy?"

"No, you're not crazy. I've known Palmer Middleton for years. He's a patron of the theater and arts department at the college. I see him from time to time at charity events. I believe he travels once a month with his wife, Rita, to Puerto Rico to visit her mother. But a few months back, his wife couldn't make the trip. She insisted that Palmer make the trip anyway to visit her family. So, on the spur of the moment, Palmer called and asked if I'd like to go and I said sure, if I could bring my friend Martha with me. He said, of course, so off we went to San Juan for the weekend. It was quite an experience—almost like being in Spain but only a three-hour flight away."

Dumbstruck, Henry mumbled, "I…I don't know what to say. Martha never told me about a trip to Puerto Rico." He sat, his eyes closed. *What does it all mean?* He looked at Britt. "Why would she not tell me of this?"

"I don't know, Henry."

"Was there anyone else on the trip?"

"No, just me, Martha, Palmer, and Jack."

"Did Jack travel around with you at all, or hang out with you?"

"No. He disappeared after we landed. We didn't see him again until we were ready to leave."

"Tell me about this Palmer Middleton. He must have money to have a private jet?"

"He's a well-known attorney, but he doesn't own the jet. His wife's father, Pedro Rodrigues, does. Palmer's hinted to me that his wife's family in Puerto Rico is very well off, and that affords Palmer to stretch his world quite a bit."

Henry didn't know where to go with all of this. He exhaled slowly.

"I've been on the job less than a week and I'm exhausted. The mental gymnastics of unrehearsed conversations on subjects you are unprepared for is debilitating for someone like me. But hearing revelations about Martha that I knew nothing of confounds me the most." He reached for the pocket of his tweed jacket and his pipe but found only his cotton polo shirt. "God, I'd love a smoke." He sighed. "And a…"

A man appeared in front of Britt. "Hey there," he said. "You're showing off those fine, long legs again, Britt."

Britt shook her head as if she'd heard this line before.

"Byron, I'd like you to meet Charlie Andrews, an old friend of mine from college. Charlie, this is Byron Rossi, who works in the theater department with me."

Henry was raising himself to get up when Byron stuck his hand out, his white teeth flashing as they shook hands. He leaned over and gave Britt a brush kiss on the cheek.

"You're more beautiful than when I last saw you an hour ago," he said, pulling a chair over and signaling for the server.

Britt came back with, "Byron, you know your sweet talk won't get you anywhere with me anymore, but it's still nice to hear."

Dressed in blue slacks and a white silk shirt unbuttoned at the top—one more button than needed—it surprised Henry how he took an instant dislike for the man. He looked to be around forty and with dark curly hair and large brown eyes. Henry thought of his resemblance to Lord Byron, possibly England's most famous poet who had once been called "mad, bad, and dangerous to know." Henry decided to sit back and observe.

Britt continued on, looking at Byron. "Tell me what's going on with Emily…that is, if you're still seeing her."

Byron acted as if Henry were not there and started right in. "Yes, I am, and I don't know what do to with her. She's beginning to act just like her mother, always questioning me about what I do and how I act. Yesterday, she lectured me on why I shouldn't drive a Hummer in Charleston." He threw up his hands in frustration. "She must have absorbed her mother's attitude after she died." He sat back and pouted.

Britt looked startled at his outburst and fired back, "For one thing, she's right to give you hell for driving a damn Hummer on these narrow streets. I think you're the only idiot who owns one and drives it around downtown." She took a deep breath, calming herself. "Now, back to what we were talking about. I've not seen any change in Emily since Martha's death other than grief. I think you're just overreacting to a bad time she's going through right now. The last thing she needs is you becoming combative with her."

"Well, you know how Martha was with Emily." He glanced at Henry for a moment, who sat staring at him, expressionless. "She told me her mother had hounded her for years over her grades, then taking off for three years to run around Mexico and beyond. It didn't sit well with her. When she decided on law school instead of English…well, that really upset Martha. I thought after she died that Emily could relax and we could finally enjoy each other. But she kept on acting just like her mother."

Henry squirmed in his seat, but merely took a deep breath and sat back. The talk of a Hummer took him back to that night when he saw one on the fourth floor of the garage. He steadied himself, knowing he could learn more from listening than making a scene.

Britt sat forward and stared at Byron. "That's enough whining about Emily and her mother. Sounds like Emily tells you what you *need* to hear, not just what you *like* to hear."

Flashing his big smile, Byron rose slowly.

"See you in class tomorrow, Britt." He shot an insolent glance at Henry before sauntering off.

"Damn, he can make me mad," she said, plopping back down in her chair. "Tomorrow, he'll act as if this conversation never took place. I'm used to this. He gets petulant at the slightest affront to his masculinity."

"He's easy to dislike," said Henry. It occurred to him that a few months ago, he would never have given such a blunt opinion on anyone. "He's a strange one," Henry mused aloud. "Walks in and begins with an almost embarrassing flattering of you. Then, in the next sentence, tells us how much he disliked Martha and was mad at Emily for being like her. Then he ends with a flippant goodbye. Is he on drugs?"

"Not that I know of, but I sometimes think he should be." She smiled at this before shaking her head in frustration. "Byron can be dark and moody at times, and…" She stopped. "I've seen him have mood swings that almost scare you for a moment. But I've worked with him for over ten years, and he's always regained his equilibrium in time so as not to affront anybody. He has a knack for the theater and acting that I've seldom witnessed. We've come to tolerate his occasional 'Mad Hatter' episodes."

Concerned, Henry slowly shook his head. "It makes me wonder why Emily is dating someone like him. But then again, she's always stretched her boundaries." With tales of Puerto Rico and now this Byron character, Henry found himself even more confused and unsettled than when he had sat down.

# CHAPTER 15

Henry realized from the start of his "do-it-yourself" detective endeavor that there was no roadmap to how to go about solving a murder. He had already seen or heard all the official information on Martha's death that was available to a layman. He would have to show up, see what happened, and take each day as it came. He had already proved this method worked when he followed Jack to the airport, simply walked into the terminal, and struck up a conversation with Sam. Then, having tea at the hotel, Britt and Byron showed up. He'd been at it a week and had learned more information than he could dissect and analyze.

He knew, at some point, he would have to talk to Jack and see what he could learn. It would be an unscripted conversation to get him talking about Martha and that night; he needed to see how Jack responded. Not that he would admit anything, but if he gave signs or raised suspicions that might somehow lead me in a direction to investigate, I might even find evidence of Jack's complicity in Martha's death. Henry believed he now had enough confidence to approach Jack.

Henry had followed Jack numerous times to an upscale sports bar on King Street that appeared to be one of his favorite hangouts. He practiced how he would start a conversation and bring up the subject of the mysterious death of a woman that he had heard about. He realized that the conversation would all be unrehearsed, and that he would have to be at his best to not be detected.

Late one afternoon, with considerable trepidation, he went to the bar dressed as "Charlie" in hopes that Jack might come in. It was a popular up-scale hangout for the locals that served fine food that, even with the muted HD TVs scattered about the walls, had a pleasant atmosphere. Soft classic rock bathed the cozy room with its polished wood bar, floor, and tables. The after-work crowd had begun to stream in when Henry spotted a few openings at the far end of the bar. He took a seat on one side of the corner, ordering a craft beer and beer nuts. The seat just around the corner was open, so Henry let his beer nuts and sunglasses drift over in front of the empty chair—in hopes of dissuading anyone from sitting there. He could see the front door from his seat and imagined seeing Jack walk in. He tried taking slow, deep breaths to slow his heartbeat. It didn't help.

Thirty minutes passed before Jack stepped in and made his way along the bar, slapping folks on the back and making jokes. As Jack walked toward him, Henry felt as if he were tied to a post watching the firing squad file out in front of him. Jack motioned to the bartender, pointing to the empty chair by Henry.

"The usual, Tommy," he said, smiling. He sat down without asking if the seat were taken.

"These must be yours," said Jack, as he nudged Henry's beer nuts and sunglasses back toward him.

"Sorry, they eased over there without me seein' 'em." Smiling, he stuck out his hand. "Name's Charlie, by the way."

"Jack," he said, and shook his hand just as the bartender set a bourbon on the rocks in front of him.

Henry looked up at the TVs. "I'm 'bout ready for football to git started. How 'bout you?" He was still looking up at the screen where the talking heads appeared to be comparing the upcoming schedules of various college teams.

Jack glanced up at the screen. "Yeah, me too," he said, studying his drink and swirling the glass in his hands. "You know, I played a little ball in college, myself. Back before there were so many rules like these days, where it's more like playing flag football."

"I guess they're just tryin' to keep people from gettin' hurt too bad." Henry didn't mean to get in a discussion over the merits of tackle football.

"Yeah, we don't want anyone to get a bloody nose, do we?" Jack looked over at Henry for the first time. "Say, aren't you the guy from the coffee shop looking for a place to stay?"

Henry's mind froze for a moment. "Uh, yeah. I was tryin' to remember where I'd seen ya before. That's it…at the coffee shop. Still stayin' with my buddy, though. That Sally sure seemed like a nice lady. Hey, weren't you wearin' some sort of uniform that day?" Henry felt like he was rambling on too much.

"Sure was. I'm a pilot and had a flight that morning. And yes, Sally's…" He stopped, looking past Henry. "Whew, look at that. She looks better every time I see her."

Henry turned and saw a stunning, dark-haired woman dressed in a white blouse and flowing tan skirt walking toward a table near the bar, where a man in a dark suit was seated. "You know her?" he asked.

"Had the pleasure of her company for a little while a few months back."

She reached the table and stood there. The man sat, unmoving, watching her as she pulled out her chair and sat down.

"Well, that fella's a real dick," said Jack, still staring at the man. "Just sat there. Didn't get up. Didn't help her get seated." Jack raised up off his seat a little, as if about to go say something to the man. But he sat back down. "What a jerk," he mumbled, taking a long pull on his drink.

"She's good lookin', that's fer sure," said Henry. "Had you been seein' her much?"

"Saw her just a few times. Right after I had to give up on this lady I'd been chasing for some time." He stopped and stared ahead a moment. "Guess you could say she was my lifelong love."

Henry sat up and looked at Jack, caught by surprise that in less than a minute he was in a conversation about Martha with a talkative Jack. He came back with a follow up question. "Don't mean to pry, but what happened? Why'd you give up on her?" Henry followed his instincts, hoping for the best—praying that Jack wouldn't recognize him.

"I'll tell you why. I found out what a conceited, superior ass she really was." He picked up his drink and finished it off.

"You musta got real mad at that?"

"Sure did," said Jack in a low voice, as he stared straight ahead, lost in memory.

"So what happened with her?" *The* question.

Jack took a moment before he was back in the present. "I don't know," he said. "She just…she just went away."

"Where'd she go? She leave town?"

"No, she didn't leave town. The police found her drowned in her car. Said she drove into the river by mistake."

Pinching the bridge of his nose, Henry took a slow sip of his beer, as if he were thinking hard.

"You know I can't figure how someone could do such a thing. How do you find a road that takes you to a river where you can just drive in till yer underwater and drowned? They got roads like that around here?"

"Actually, it was a ramp into the river where folks can launch their boats. She drove down it by mistake in a bad rainstorm we were having one night."

"Gosh, I never heard of such a thing. So nobody was tryin' to rob her or there was nothin' crazy goin' on?"

"Guess not. The police checked it all out and said it was an accident." He paused, a frown on his face. Then, with a big grin, he turned toward Charlie. "But I found a replacement! Didn't take me long at all." He signaled Tommy for a refill and another beer for Henry.

"You mean, you lost one love then acquired another just like that? Jeez, that's somethin'."

Jack looked at him, quizzically. "I used to know someone who would use a word like that, but I can't remember who it is right now."

Caught by surprise, Henry didn't know what word he had used. "Which word you talkin' about?"

Jack stared at him. "Acquired. You said I *acquired* another love."

Almost without hesitation, Henry came up with, "My ma hammered that one word in me in high school and how to use it. Said it'd make me smart. Had to use it in a sentence three times durin' dinner every evenin'. Acquired, acquired, acquired. Don't think it worked, but I can't seem to forget it." Smiling, he held his breath while staring at Jack, willing him to buy his explanation.

Jack chuckled. "I know what you mean." Henry exhaled, while Jack continued. "My father quizzed me every day on sports. Said it would carry me a long way. Don't know about that, but I make enough that I can still buy my own drinks." He glanced over at the table with the lady. "That son of a bitch," he murmured under his breath.

Henry looked over and saw the woman talking to the man, who now had a big grin on his face. He's looking at Jack.

Jack slid off his chair and sauntered over to them. He leaned on the table, staring at the man. "You got a problem?" he asked, louder than he needed to.

"No, but I hear you do," the man replied, the smile still on his face.

Nearby tables were taking notice, while Henry guessed what was about to happen. The dark-haired lady put her hand on the man's forearm as if to warn him. She then whispered in his ear.

"Why don't we step outside and discuss what's on your mind," said Jack.

"I think not. I haven't heard a cheap threat like that since high school."

Jack tipped the man's beer glass over. The golden liquid headed for the edge of the table and onto the man's pants.

The man pushed back from the table. He stared at Jack for a second before he stood and turned to his date. "Let's get out of here. It's not worth getting into to a fight with this guy."

"Just a minute, if you don't mind," said Jack in a slow, level voice. "A little advice before you run off."

The man stopped, now on guard.

"Hang around her a while and you'll have the same problem I had. Women like her enjoy going along for the ride until they decide to erase you off the board and move on."

"Jesus, now this guy's giving therapy sessions," said the man as he took his date by the arm and led her out.

Jack stepped back to the bar, dropped a couple of twenties, and then walked out without another word. Henry noticed that some of the people nearby were smiling, while others looked puzzled.

Henry's shoulders slumped as he relaxed from one of the most intense encounters he had experienced in some time. While he sipped on his beer, he was lost in thought, pleased that as Charlie, he had faced Jack Townsend up close, in a bar, and elicited as much information as he could have hoped for—without being recognized or getting in a fight. He tried to identify what he had learned, if anything, from his short talk before it was interrupted by Jack's antics. Jack had been straightforward in recounting the cause of Martha's death, but he gave no real clues that he may have been involved. The advice Jack gave to the man may have said the most. That his "lifelong love" had erased him off the board and moved on. Did he get revenge in the heat of the moment?

But Henry felt somewhat baffled by Jack's reaction to the man who had laughed at him. Apparently, Jack had assumed what it was, and the man's flippant answer confirmed it. It appeared that Jack was embarrassed but Henry couldn't think of what would set him off like that. He thought, Britt might have some insight. While it was still fresh in his mind, he called her and said he was nearby in a bar. He then asked if he could stop by for a minute.

---

Henry rang her doorbell, still dressed as a tourist. When the door opened,

Britt exclaimed, "Have you been out on the town during happy hour? As Charlie?"

"Yep, been talkin' to Jack at a bar," said Henry, straight-faced. "He's upset, and I sure could use a drink."

Britt's eyes widened. "What? You didn't! Get yourself inside right now."

As Henry stepped in, Britt brushed by him and took a quick look around outside. Stepping back in, she shut the door. "Hey, he's mad, but not at me," said Henry. "That's what I wanted to talk to you about."

Henry recounted what had just happened at the sports bar and the success of his first meeting with Jack as Charlie.

"Jack told me about losing his lifelong love and what a bitch she turned out to be. I could tell he was heating up just thinking back on it. Then he said that she just went away and told an unemotional account in a few sentences of how she drowned. Then, wearing a big grin, he finished by saying he'd already found a replacement. A few minutes later, he tried to start a fight with a man at a nearby table with his date."

As Henry told the story, Britt nodded like she knew the answer.

"I've done some checking with some of my friends who have dated Jack more recently and I think I found an answer to his son, Patrick, following Emily. It might also answer your question about what just happened at the bar. Patrick, Jack's only child, has been estranged from him since Jack's divorce some years ago…his wife took Patrick to San Francisco. Patrick is gay and Jack's had a problem accepting this. He has a phobia that he didn't produce a 'normal' boy. He worries about his manhood to the point that he has trouble performing in bed sometimes. After five years in California, Patrick showed up in town a few months back. I think Jack's anxiety is heightened by having his gay son in front of him on a daily basis."

Henry shook his head. "This is all becoming more intriguing than I imagined," he mumbled.

Britt continued. "So, according to my friends, when he fails in bed he gets embarrassed. I'll bet the lady in the bar was telling her date about Jack's shortcomings in the bedroom and Jack picked up on it. His manhood was being questioned in public and, for Jack, that's worth a fight any time."

"I guess that all makes sense," said Henry, "especially with his temperament. It doesn't take much to set him off. But how does Patrick following Emily fit into all of this?"

"This is just a hunch, but ask Emily if she only spots Patrick when she's with Byron."

Henry made a quick call to Emily, who confirmed that it was generally the case.

Nodding, Britt smiled. "Byron has been known to occasionally have a boyfriend. I would bet that Patrick is following Byron, not Emily. Byron *is* a pretty boy, as is Patrick, for that matter."

Henry dropped his head. "Jesus, there ain't nothin' just straight up 'round here, is there?"

# CHAPTER 16

A few days later, Emily surprised Henry with a late afternoon call that Byron had just called her for a dinner date that evening and that maybe Patrick would show up. Henry had not told her yet what he and Britt had guessed— that he could be following Byron, not her. He had no idea what he might say to Patrick, if he saw him. He'd ask him why he was following Emily. He'd deny it and that would probably be the end of it. But Henry had found since coming to Charleston that seemingly innocuous meetings and conversations could provide bits of valuable information in solving the puzzle he was committed to solving.

Dressed casually as a tourist as when he met Byron at the hotel lounge, Henry waited in the bar area sipping a beer and eating peanuts. Emily and Byron appeared at the front door, and he watched Emily steer Byron to a high-top table in the bar area not far from him. They ordered drinks and an appetizer. Soon after, a young man fitting Emily's description of Patrick wandered in, looked around, and took a seat at a table next to Henry.

Nervous, thinking he would be recognized by Byron, Henry worked hard at not looking his way or showing any interest. He could overhear most of their conversation, as they were talking louder than normal. Byron was on the same subject of his dissatisfaction with Emily acting like her mother.

"I think you're glad she's dead, Byron!" said Emily, starting to stand.

"Well, she won't be hammering on you any longer now, will she?"

"I can't believe I'm hearing this. I've had enough of you!" She turned to leave when Byron grabbed her by the arm. She yanked it free and strode toward the door. Byron pushed his seat back, threw some cash on the table, and followed her out. It all happened so fast that Henry was slow to react. Unsure of what to do but concerned for Emily's safety, he threw a twenty-dollar bill on the table and walked outside. He spotted her crossing the street at the corner, with Byron just off to her side talking to her excitedly. Emily stared straight ahead. Henry turned toward the crosswalk to follow them and bumped into the young man from the bar, who had silently appeared beside him.

Henry stared at him. His nose looked as if it had been recently broken.

"Who are you? And why are you watching them?" he demanded, surprised at his abrupt manner.

"I'm Patrick," he said simply.

Henry was startled at his reply. He wasn't sure what to say or do, so he stepped around him and hurried to cross the street.

He was now a block behind them but was able to maintain that distance by walking as fast as he could. He wasn't sure where Emily was heading but assumed it was to her apartment.

He saw them enter the house and the lights go on. Within a few minutes, Henry was on the sidewalk out front. The living room shutters were open. He saw Emily and Byron standing in front of one of the armchairs. They were arguing. Suddenly, Byron pushed her. She fell into the chair. Reaching over, she grabbed a small vase of flowers on the side table and threw it, hitting him on the shoulder. Surprised, he bent over and picked up a small vase off a side table.

Henry found himself unable to move or take any action. He just stood there, staring—waiting for the drama to play out.

Byron raised the vase above his head and hurled it against the wall behind Emily. She walked up close to him and said something. Turning, he headed for the door. Henry all but sprinted around the corner and across the street before Byron came out.

Henry found a bench to sit and calm his heart. Shame and embarrassment for his lack of courage to at least try and protect his daughter swept over him. He also thought of his inaction with Patrick in front of the restaurant. He concluded, I've failed miserably on all counts. He felt he should go back and console Emily, but she was stronger than he was. Besides, he was ashamed to admit he just stood there and watched.

But he had to confess his inaction. He called Britt and asked if he might stop by again.

———

Britt opened the door. Her smile greeted him, and he felt safe, glad she was there to listen and to understand. The smell of food cooking flooded over his sagging shoulders, making him feel better. Henry sat down as she brought him a glass of wine saying there was enough dinner for them both—"if you'd like to stay." He didn't argue. He was happy just to be there with her, comforted. He told her what had happened, what he had failed to do. He grunted, embarrassed again at his inability to act—my Achilles heel.

"You shouldn't take it so hard. No one got hurt because you failed to rescue the maiden. Remember, you have not encountered these types of situations before. I doubt you ever threw anything at Martha and had to deal with her reaction."

"That's true. I can only imagine what she would have done if I had." He needed to ask her a question. "Do you think Byron could have had a hand in Martha's death? He's acted about half crazy both times I've been near him. He directs a lot of anger at Martha and shows little regret that she died."

"I've worked with him for years. He's moody and difficult to get along with. I've also seen him short tempered. He would explode at a student actor or actress over minor issues. But it's a long leap from that type of behavior to killing someone. I believe he's in love with Emily, and I knew Martha well enough to know that she didn't approve of him. I saw her tell him to his face that he wasn't good enough for Emily. I thought he would explode. His face turned red, and he stood there, his fists clenched. But he only turned and walked away. Byron doesn't like hearing talk like that, as I think you saw the other day at the hotel lounge. I tried to calm the waters between the two, but Martha would not concede an inch in her assessment of some of Emily's boyfriends."

Henry shook his head. "I never realized Martha could be so overbearing with Emily."

"Martha could be difficult, there's no question about that. I grew up with her and she was accustomed to having it her way. I think her family money and her father's position warped her sense of values somewhat. But she could also be generous. She helped me through some financial hardships, and I owed her a lot for helping me become who I am today."

"I could see back in college that you two had almost become sisters. And it carried on, as it seemed she never went more than a few months without coming to Charleston for a visit or convention of some sort. I think she always felt more at home here than in Asheville."

"Well, she grew up here and she loved going to the beach. Although that scare we had a few months ago reminded her that it's not always sun, sand, and umbrella drinks."

"What scare was that? She never mentioned anything to me about any scare at the beach."

"She got caught in a rip tide. I had to go out and save her. But at one point, I got so tired I thought I would have to let her go." She shook her head, whispering, "To save myself." She chuckled. "For once, I was in charge of Martha."

Puzzled, Henry wondered why Martha never told him about this. It's not something you would easily forget. "Martha was lucky you used to be a beach lifeguard, although it sounds like you were on the edge, saving Martha."

"You forget how the ocean can sneak up on you without warning. Plus, I'm not eighteen anymore." She rubbed the bridge of her nose and sighed. "I forgot about dinner."

She walked to the stove while Henry got up and walked around the living room, casually looking at the modern art on the walls. He came to stop in front of a smaller print, placed in a corner. It was of a couple in a red sports car with the wind in their hair; they were driving on a road overlooking a beach and the ocean. It reminded him of the picture in his study that he and Martha envisioned themselves doing in the English countryside. He swallowed hard as tears formed in his eyes. He stared at it. Straightening up, he wiped his eyes and returned to the counter. He sat down, took a sip of his drink, and returned to their conversation.

"I wish I had come with her to Charleston more often than I did. It would have broadened my view of life, being away from the college. I didn't realize how much I had morphed into the typical stuffy professor. Gosh, I've never been out of the country. If I'd been down here a few months ago, maybe I could have gone to Puerto Rico with you and Martha? I think that would have been exciting."

Britt set their dinner on the counter. "I assume you like Italian. I know Martha did."

Henry was still in Puerto Rico. "Talk about being in a new country, did Palmer take you to some fine restaurants?"

"Well, unfortunately, I caught a bug and an upset stomach right after we arrived, so I ended up eating soup and crackers most of the time at the hotel which, by the way, Rita's father, Pedro Rodrigues, owns. Palmer did take Martha out two nights to restaurants and showed her around the sights. They surprised Rita's father the second evening at his restaurant when they joined him for dinner. Pedro was quite the gentleman. He seemed to know everyone in the restaurant. But Martha told me later that she could tell he was upset at Palmer."

"Did she say why?" asked Henry, curious as to why she would pick up on this.

"Well, Martha guessed it was two things. Initially, it was Pedro's surprise and questioning look on his face at having her there rather than his daughter, Rita. She said his expression softened when he asked her polite questions about her background and parents, but she noticed his demeanor seemed to tighten again when she told him her father had been the DA in Charleston during the time of the white-collar drug smuggling in South Carolina in the '70s. The second thing that affected her was a slight disturbance later at their table that Martha witnessed. She said a well-dressed man came to the table and whispered in Pedro's ear. Pedro then stood and motioned to a man by the door, who came over and escorted him out. Pedro apologized to Martha and said the man was delirious. Martha told me she understood two words the man muttered as he was escorted away. The man had said, 'fucking drogas,' and even I know what that means. She said Pedro apologized for the interruption again, but he was less friendly afterward. She caught him glaring at Palmer as he paid for dinner with five one-hundred-dollar bills."

Henry squirmed in his chair when he heard the word "drogas." He also wondered why Martha never told him about this whole trip to Puerto Rico. It didn't make sense to him unless she wanted to hide her evening dinners with Palmer.

Henry couldn't help but feel upset and jealous about his wife out alone with a rich attorney and his father-in-law on an island in the Caribbean.

"Sounds like Martha was knee-deep in money and influence in Puerto Rico. Does Pedro own other real estate in San Juan?"

"I'm not sure, but since Jack started flying for them earlier this year, he's bought a new car, a new boat, and just recently a condo downtown in the French Quarter, which is high-dollar country. His flying time with Air Carolinas has been erratic, he told me. So, I guess his part-time flying for Palmer must be paying off in spades since he's 'movin' on up,' so to speak."

Henry wished he had a scorecard to keep up with all this.

"Well, a few days after we got back," said Britt, "I got a call from Palmer, who told me Rita found out who he took on the trip to Puerto Rico. She was more than a little upset, mainly for taking Martha and myself on her father's plane—but more so for taking Martha to dinner and meeting Pedro. Rita said it had embarrassed Pedro that his daughter's husband was out on the town, in his restaurant, with a strange woman."

Henry got up and walked around the living room, deep in thought. "You know, it may not be a stretch that you could make the case that this Pedro guy deals in drugs," he said.

"And Palmer knows that Martha's father was the DA," said Britt, "when drugs were being hustled into South Carolina by the so-called 'white-collar' smugglers. Martha told me some hair-raising stories that her father told her about the smuggling during that time. I'll bet soon after that trip, Pedro was brought up to speed on Martha's background on the drug trade. Plus, here's his son-in-law squiring this lady around in front of him, showing her off. All this might, well…piss Pedro off."

"This whole thing pisses *me* off," said Henry. "Could all this have anything to do with Martha's death?" He fell into a chair. "Jesus, I'm beginning to think I never knew Martha."

# CHAPTER 17

Henry had talked on the phone every week with George Holland in Asheville with updates on his progress, but still felt he needed some extra help. He had been successful being a "tourist" around Jack, Byron, and Sam, but if he was to try and talk to Palmer Middleton, an attorney, he needed coaching on how he might go about it. He called George and asked if he would bring his PI up to speed on what he had in mind, that perhaps they could set up a conference call.

Henry felt he needed to stop, take a deep breath, and regroup. He had decided to summarize where he was with his investigation and had bought a large whiteboard to track the timeline between the retirement banquet and the discovery of her body: Who was where, what they said, etcetera. Also, a notebook of his discoveries, ideas, guesses, assumptions, suspects, motivations, gut feelings on all the people in his circle of study. He kept a separate journal for what he had learned about Martha, along with his thoughts and reactions and how her actions may or may not have contributed to her own death.

He would have to satisfy himself, beyond a reasonable doubt, that the pilot was at fault for Martha's death. Jack had the opportunity, the motive, and the method. Although in the past few weeks, two other possible suspects, to a lesser degree, had surfaced. Byron Rossi, the Mad Hatter, had shown his dislike for Martha to the point that he was glad she was in the ground, and his Hummer was still in the garage after Martha's car was gone. He saw her leave from the party and could have easily found out where they were going to eat. And now, the revelations that Martha was in Puerto Rico with Palmer, and had dinner in San Juan with Pedro Rodriguez, a local tycoon with a thirty-five-million-dollar jet and two hotels, and who may be connected with drugs. Palmer knew of Martha's probable knowledge of drug running from hearing stories from her father. Could this add up to enough evidence that she picked up that Pedro was possibly in the drug business? It might be enough circumstantial reason for her to be taken out before she publicly commented on it. Killing her the way she died is not beyond the realm of possibilities for a drug cartel; they're more sophisticated than machine guns these days. They would have to have advance warning she was in town, some background info on where she might eat and that she most probably would go alone to get the car. Palmer and Martha, two Charlestonians, had spent enough time together in Puerto Rico trading stories for Palmer to learn that her father was the DA of Charleston during the "white-collar" drug days in Charleston. And Henry, knowing Martha, figured she probably expanded on her knowledge.

Henry now had three suspects, with varying degrees of probability: Jack, Byron, and Palmer/Pedro. At the moment, he was concerned with Palmer and Pedro, and whether they had been worried about Martha realizing how Palmer and his wife's extravagant living expenses were financed. Also, Jack's increase in "toys" at the same time his regular job had slackened off. If so, they were probably capable of killing Martha before she spoke up about it and making it look like an accident.

Henry stopped. Standing, he looked around, as if to confirm where he was. He sat back down. It had occurred to him that if he were thinking like this back in Asheville, in his study, and told George about Martha and Puerto Rico and his suspicions, George would have called the hospital to come and get him.

Henry wondered if he'd fallen off track in his thinking. All these revelations about Martha and the consequences of her actions had his brain muddled. The preciseness of his daily living for decades had not sufficiently prepared him for the new stories about Martha he was hearing on a daily basis—on top of trying to solve a possible murder. The old Henry was still alive.

Henry tried to figure out how someone could intercept Martha and get her to drive into the water without any sign of physical abuse.

He read up on Jack, who was in special ops in the service. One thing they learned in special ops is the use of pressure points that can knock a person out for a short period of time, leaving no physical marks on the person. He would be able to get in the car with her and get close enough to do this before she put up a fight. No one else could. Plus, he was the only one who knew when she left the restaurant and where she was going. Nobody else could foresee the circumstances that would put her in the garage at that particular time and have a way to get her into the water without a trace of interference. Everything points to Jack. Henry considered whether he should talk to anybody else about his theories. How might someone pull this off? The police, an investigator? No, this is my deal to figure out.

At ten o'clock, George called on a three-way connection with Henry and the private investigator. Henry gave them a summary of his clues on how he got to the point of considering Palmer as a valid suspect. They talked for an hour, and Henry came away with a plan for an initial conversation with Palmer.

Both the PI and George stressed to Henry that, "If he decides to do this, he'll either get thrown out for wasting Palmer's time on a ridiculous accusation coming from a person unknown to him…or, if you're hitting a sensitive spot, Palmer will probably listen longer to see just how much you know and how close you are to the truth. And remember, Henry, if you're on target, and they consider you a threat, you may end up like Martha."

This sounds like a TV drama, but they're mainly based on true life incidents. Henry was given some examples of how a conversation might proceed and how to answer with different responses from Palmer. Henry told them that he had enough to give it a try.

All he needed was the address of Palmer's office and the internet could supply that in a minute or less. But he needed to find it himself and figured if he went to the executive airport and chatted with Sam, there was no telling what other information he might get.

# CHAPTER 18

Dressed in his Chicago Bears ball hat, a multicolored Hawaiian shirt, shorts, and sneakers, Henry drove out to the airport late one morning to see if he could find a way to get in front of Palmer Middleton for a chat. As he pulled up to park, he spotted Palmer's father-in-law's dark blue jet across the tarmac parked in a line with six other private jets. Standing by the fence, he hoped to find another jet preparing for takeoff. He remembered on his last trip here being captivated by the preflight preparations, then hearing their engines building to a crescendo as they began their roll down the runway before jumping into another environment. He smiled, imagining himself in the cockpit of that jet with his own preparation for takeoff and rolling down the interstate at excess speeds before jumping into the air. His shoulders slumped when he saw the runway empty.

Inside, he saw Sam behind a counter looking at a computer screen while a young dark-haired girl sat at a small computer desk. Another young man polished the floor.

Sam looked up as he approached. He smiled. "Are you back to sign up for a ride? It's Charlie, isn't it?"

"Yup, Sam, it is. Been thinkin' a lot about this. I'd like to take a ride in that jet that goes to Porta Rica. Got the money with me right now." He pulled his wallet out of his back pocket and slapped it down on the counter.

"Well, Charlie, you can only get a ride on that particular jet with an invitation from the owner." Sam leaned back with a grin on his face, as if anticipating an entertaining conversation about to get underway.

"Sam, why don't we just give 'em a quick call and see if he'll give me one?"

Chuckling, Sam shook his head. "I sure wish it was that easy, but the owner would need to meet you and interview you about why you want a ride in his jet instead of flying commercial."

"Can't we git all that done over the phone?" asked Charlie, frowning.

"Afraid not, Charlie."

"How 'bout I go down to where he's at and see 'em?" Charlie's eyebrows rose up, as if this was a grand idea.

"That might be difficult, as I'm sure his schedule stays pretty booked up."

"Say, what if I just go and wait?" asked Charlie, his voice rising at the possibility he'd just solved the problem.

"Could give that a try, I guess," said Sam, struggling to hold back a smile.

"Where you figure he's at today?"

"At his office, I would think. I'll write down his address for you."

"That'd be great." He slapped the counter at the problem solved and grabbed his wallet.

"Here you go. And Charlie, tell him you got his address off the internet."

"Gotcha, Sam. I'll tell 'em that." Henry winked. "Only you and me will know where I got it."

"Good luck, Charlie. Let me know how it works out."

"Thanks, Sam. I owe you one." He reached out, his hand held high, palm facing out, and Sam gave him a high five. "All right!" said Henry, turning and hustling out the front door.

In his car, Henry punched the address into his phone and headed for his apartment. He needed to change into the clothes he had purchased days before. They were more appropriate for talking to an attorney than in his Hawaiian shirt and sneakers. He would become attorney Charles Anderson, Esq. from Anderson & Associates, Chicago. He had a minimum number of business cards printed up with a bogus street address and telephone number. He figured he'd be finished and out the door before anyone decided to check his identification.

———

Dressed in a three-piece dark gray suit and carrying a slim leather briefcase, Henry walked into the law firm of Middleton & Associates. He told the receptionist his name was Charles Anderson, he did not have an appointment, but needed to see Mr. Middleton concerning his father-in-law, Mr. Rodrigues. Henry waited less than ten minutes before being escorted into the office of Palmer Middleton.

Surrounded by walls of glistening leather-bound books and a view of the harbor, Palmer rose from a cherry desk that could easily seat twelve for dinner. He came around to shake hands. Silver-haired and dressed in a crisp white shirt and college tie, Palmer looked as if he were ready to shoot a commercial for the American Bar Association.

"Palmer Middleton," he said. "Nice to meet you, Mr. Anderson. Please have a seat and tell me what's on your mind." He returned to his seat, sat back, and smiled.

Henry sat, setting his briefcase beside him. "Mr. Middleton, I've come here representing a friend of mine, a Mrs. Martha Willis, who recently died in a mysterious accident here in town a few months ago. You might remember her as she accompanied you, along with another woman, to San Juan, Puerto Rico, about four months ago."

The smile disappeared. Palmer looked at him, stone-faced.

"Who are you and why are you here?"

"And you took Mrs. Willis to dinner both nights you were in town. The second night, Pedro Rodrigues joined you for dinner. Am I on target so far, Mr. Middleton?"

Palmer had not moved.

"To continue, I believe Mr. Rodrigues was kind enough to pay for the dinners and drinks with five, hundred-dollar bills. Sadly, for you, I'm sure Mrs. Willis had to return to her hotel room alone, as you were obligated to stay with your father-in-law. So far so good?"

There was still no movement from Palmer.

"I'm sure your wife, Rita, is aware of all this, and you have already had to answer for your actions that weekend. I would venture a guess that Martha Willis was not invited over for dinner at your place."

Silence.

"But we find it strange that shortly after her return from this trip, she drove her car down the Third Avenue boat ramp one evening into the water and drowned. And of all things, it was ruled an accident. From your time with Mrs. Willis, did she strike you as the type of person that could do such a thing?"

Palmer straightened up, sat tall, and found his voice.

"I don't know what you're trying to insinuate, but I want you out of my office immediately…or I'll call security." He stood and leaned on his desk, staring at Henry.

Henry rose slowly, picked up his briefcase, and smiled. "No need for that. I learned what I came here for. Good day." He let himself out.

———

Over dinner at Britt's that evening, Henry recounted the day's adventures as "Charlie" and "Charles."

"I must say, you took your impersonations up a notch or two when you went to Palmer's office. Not to mention what might have happened if you had not extracted yourself out of there when you did." She shook her head. "I know Palmer and he gives the appearance of just another dapper, silver-haired lawyer, but I've heard how he can cut someone's legs off and have them in jail before they know what's happened. You're lucky you slipped out. You caught him by surprise with your story and had him squirming over how you knew details of the dinner with Pedro and Martha. Your assertion that he might know something about Martha driving down the ramp into the water pulled the plug on the conversation. I'm a little amazed that he let you walk out of there."

"Why? What could he have done?"

"He could have had you arrested on some trumped-up charge. Enough to find out your name is not Charles Anderson. He could have had you spending the evening explaining to the police why you tricked your way into his office and how you came about such detailed information on his activities during a visit to his father-in-law in Puerto Rico. It could have been a real mess, Henry."

"Jeez, I never thought about all that."

"I was the only one, other than Martha, who could have known that Pedro was throwing hundred-dollar bills around. So, one of us had to have told you. I bet I'll have a call from Palmer tomorrow, asking me about Charles Anderson."

"You could tell him that you don't know a Charles Anderson and that he must have gotten that specific information from Martha before she died. She might have told her husband, but she didn't even tell him she'd been to Puerto Rico." Henry stopped to think for a moment. "I see what you mean. It comes back to you." He put his hand on top of hers. "I'm sorry, Britt. The last thing I wanted to do was to drag you into this."

"It would be interesting to learn what Jack has seen and heard on his travels with Palmer and Rita." She slid her hand out from beneath Henry's and stood.

"Here we are talking about Palmer maybe being implicated in Martha's death, and we're about ready to ask Jack what *he* thinks of all this." Patting Henry on the shoulder, she stepped over to the wine bottle, came back, and replenished their glasses.

"Did *anyone* kill Martha?" she asked. "Are we chasing our tails here? Do we have a real clue from Jack? A real clue from Palmer? From Byron? A real clue from *anyone*? Maybe I should investigate you, Henry, and you investigate me. I don't think Emily would kill her own mother, no matter how hard Martha rode her. Are we trying too hard here and missing the obvious?"

"When you spell it out like that, it makes us sound like just what we are—English lit nerds. Maybe we can have Jack help us with the production of *Othello*, and Palmer with the stage design just to even out the odds?" Henry took a large swallow of wine before setting his glass down. "I'm going to search Martha's car one more time for a clue…and take a car mechanic with me. Someone who knows cars better than I."

# CHAPTER 19

Henry had learned Jack had a fishing boat at a dry storage downtown, so he would have known about the boat ramp, where it was, and that it was almost finished. He would have also known that the gates were not in place yet. Henry needed to find a clue that put Jack in the car that night. He remembered his first visit to the salvage yard, where he had become more upset than he anticipated and did not put in a very good search of the car. He would go again. This time, he would take some help along, maybe like a mechanic, to help search the car more thoroughly. He texted Britt to see if she could point him toward someone who might be able to help, possibly someone who had worked around salvage cars that had been submerged. Britt called back a few hours later with a name. Henry set up a meeting with him to go to the salvage yard.

The mechanic was a young, thin man with a hard face that looked as if he had been in a few fights in his life. He had worked around salvage cars that had been submerged. He jumped in.

"My name's Johnny. Mind if I have a smoke?" he asked, pulling a cigarette from a pack of Marlboros.

Henry glanced over. "No, go right ahead. Just crack the window a bit."

They headed for North Charleston and the salvage yard. Henry gave Johnny a summary of what had happened and why they were going to the car. Johnny said he'd been around cars that had been submerged, mostly folks who had driven into a lake or deep canal late at night after being out on the town drinking. He said he'd read about the lady who drove down the boat ramp downtown a few months back.

Today, Henry's anxiety was elevated, along with his expectations. As they neared the salvage yard, he felt his heart pounding. He found the car where he had last seen it and stopped fifty feet away to stare at it. It looked no different from when he saw it a month ago, other than the surrounding weeds that had grown to the windows. Henry got out and shuffled over to it. He lowered himself into the seat behind the wheel. Johnny followed and got in the passenger side. Henry told him he was going to talk through what might have happened and to speak up if anything he said was not plausible.

He sat motionless for a minute, as he imagined himself driving to the boat ramp on a stormy night with heavy rain. He thought of what Martha might have been thinking during her last moments.

"I can't see out of the front windshield. I was sitting in the car in the garage and now I'm still in the car, but my window is down and it's raining on my face and my feet are wet and I'm too tired to move. I'm not sure where I am, and I feel rain and smell salt water. Am I in a lake, the river, the harbor? What happened? Jesus, now I feel water rising up my legs. I try to open the door, but it won't budge. Now the water is beginning to flow through the window! But I'm still strapped in my seat belt and the water's at my waist! And I can't unbuckle my seat belt! There's someone else in the car. They're just sitting there. Now the water is almost at my chin, and I can't stop it. Oh God!"

Exhausted, his head fell back against the head restraint. He glanced over at Johnny, who was outside the car on his knees looking in, his eyes wide, gripping the door at the open window.

"I was there," he muttered, "in the car with you, until the water got to your legs, then I bailed out through the open window. I feel sorry for you because you couldn't have been ready for this, never having gone through the steps, in your mind, to get out of a sinking car."

Johnny got back in the car and said, "Mind if I have another smoke to ease down?'

Henry hadn't had a cigarette since college, but if he ever needed one, it was now.

"Sure, Johnny, if you'll let me have one with you."

Johnny passed him one and they lit up. Henry inhaled and coughed, not sure this was such a good idea. Johnny exhaled a cloud out the window.

"A car will float for a short time and the electrics will work," he said, "before the water starts getting in, which gives you time to put the windows down. I must say your wife was on her toes to put the windows down so quickly. But unfortunately, sitting behind the steering wheel and trying to open the door and unfasten her seat belt with the water rising so fast made it difficult for her to get out in time."

Martha was on top of her game right to the end, thought Henry.

His head dropped in

grief.

They began their search of the car. Henry felt proud of himself for bringing a flashlight, a small tool kit, and a disposable camera to record his examination. The glove compartment was empty, as were the door pockets. He had been given all their contents by the police. He examined the front seat, a bench seat just like in the old cars, with a gear shift on the steering column. But where's Fluffy's harness? How did I miss this the other day?

Not knowing what he was looking for, they began to methodically search every square inch beginning in the front seat area. They pulled out the now moldy floor mats, looked around the pedals and up under the dashboard the best they could. Henry pulled down the sun visors—nothing. There was nothing on the top of the dash, instrument panel, steering column. He looked under the backrest looking for quarters but found no change. He had Johnny help him take out the front seat. After a brief struggle, they managed to extract the seat and had a clear view of the floor below. Nothing but a ballpoint pen and a small dead fish. They flipped over the bench seat and saw what looked to be a dirty rag caught in the webbing on the bottom of the seat, and he took a picture. They pulled it out and threw it into a bucket they had brought to carry anything of importance they might find. They continued their search into the backseat area and the trunk—nothing. They opened the hood and looked all through the engine area, then into the wheel wells and under the car. Disappointed that a clue of some sort was not found, Henry started back. When he dropped Johnny off on his way back through North Charleston, they shook hands. Henry then gave him two twenties.

Back in his room, he washed the handkerchief under a spigot of water. In less than a minute, it became evident it wasn't a rag but a smooth cloth. Excitedly, Henry continued washing it with soap until he saw the light blue color of what looked to be a handkerchief. The letters *JT* sewn in white on one corner became legible. His hands trembled as he held it up to the light.

# CHAPTER 20

With Jack's handkerchief in his pocket, Henry felt like a weight had been lifted from his shoulders. He had begun to think he would never find any proof that Jack had killed Martha. Although other suspects had surfaced, he knew all along it was Jack. By God, I've got him! A quiet celebration was called for, and what better place to do this than with a glass of cognac at the Old English Club on Queen Street. Henry had discovered it a month ago. It reminded him of where the first thought came to him, in the solitude of his own study, to take on this journey. It was only fitting to celebrate the closing of the circle in the solitude of the Old English Club.

Unknown to most tourists unless stumbled upon by accident, "The Club" had been a quiet meeting place for business professionals and the like for seventy years. Its dark, sedated interior with paneled walls, book-laden shelves, heavy furniture, and plush rugs created an atmosphere for quiet, private conversations.

A light drizzle had begun in late afternoon, with the low-hanging clouds and unseasonably cool wind. Along the narrow street, Henry—dressed casually—had a bounce in his step with the hint of an early autumn. He opened the heavy wood door and smiled. A few overstuffed armchairs surrounding a small cherry table near a corner caught his eye. He spoke to the waiter beside the bar and walked over to one of the armchairs, sitting down with a sound of contentment. Once the waiter delivered his glass of Courvoisier, he felt at home.

The club began to fill with businessmen and women. Soon, most all the chairs were taken other than the two in his corner. Henry was enjoying the atmosphere, his cognac, and just people watching.

A half hour later, Henry watched as two men dressed in sport coats walked in and headed for the bar to find all the chairs taken. Looking around, they noticed that there were two chairs near Henry. They walked over, asking if they might sit there. Henry gestured for them to sit.

John and Harold introduced themselves. Before long, they were all engrossed in sports talk with a sprinkling of politics. As hors d'oeuvres were served, all three appeared to become the best of friends.

An hour later, John and Harold decided to go to a restaurant called Henry's that was a little livelier that served dinner food and local entertainment. As they were heading for Henry's namesake, Henry was enticed to follow. Within a couple of blocks, they arrived. They found a table, food, and more to drink. The dining room and lounge were packed, with a four-piece band playing classic rock beside the small dance floor.

In high spirits, Henry was caught off guard when one of the men went to a table and invited three ladies to join them. All were attractive, well-dressed, middle-aged women and the two men moved additional chairs to the table. Henry stood and first-name introductions were attempted, although the background noise drowned out the names. Janice was standing beside Henry, and when they sat down, she put her hand on his knee. His knee jumped at the surprise. He looked at Janice with a frown. She smiled, showing perfect teeth, and pushed a blond curl from her forehead.

She leaned in close. "You really should tell me your name again."

"Henry," he croaked, not moving.

"So, now it's Henry. Then you must be the owner and it's my lucky night."

Henry was overwhelmed and feeling discombobulated from both his drinking and her hand. "Gosh," he said, and was unable to think of what to say next.

"Gosh," she repeated. "I haven't heard that word since…maybe high school." She cocked her head, looking at him. "That's cute of you to say."

Having said only two words since Janice took a seat, Henry tried a short sentence. "Would you like something to drink?"

"Maybe later, thank you. Tell me, Henry, what brings you to town, other than to check on your nightclub?" She gave his knee a squeeze, a smile crossing her face.

Henry jumped again. "Jeez, I…I guess I'm just visiting." He didn't have the energy nor mental acuity at the moment to attempt an explanation that he was not the owner of Henry's.

"Well, this town is known for its hospitality. You having a good time so far?"

"Not really." He wasn't sure where to go with this and his sharp mind was somewhat fuzzy. He heard only a muffled buzz from the rest of the table. They all seemed busy with each other.

"Well, tell me, did you fly in on your own private jet?"

"My private jet?" His eyes closed. He could almost feel himself sitting in one, as the jet rolled down the runway, the roar filling his head…and then jumping into the air, taking his breath away. Swaying in his seat, his eyes popped open. He looked at her and was, for a moment, unsure of where he was. And who is she?

"My private jet," he stated. He was still sitting in it.

"I'll bet you flew into the airport over on Johns Island," said Janice.

"Yup. Know where that is." He thought that was what she asked him.

"And I'll bet you talked to Sam."

"Sam? Sure did. Nice guy."

"Did you go talk to someone else after you talked to Sam?"

Henry was getting tired from the questions. It took too much thought to answer them. "Nope. Went home. Changed clothes."

"And I'll bet you got all dressed up in your best three-piece suit."

"Yup." He was so tired that all he wanted to do was go home and lie down.

"Well, Charlie, where'd you go next?"

Henry closed his eyes, then opened them wide, trying to stop the roar of the engines. His head cleared just enough. He managed to push himself upright and stood, looking down at Janice. His eyes half open, he smiled. "You tell Palmer he best not try to fuck with ol' Charlie." He stumbled off through the crowd.

# CHAPTER 21

The following morning, Henry was buried deep in his bed. He was awakened by the insistent ringing of his cell phone. Not sure where it might be, he stretched his arm out to the nightstand and tried to grab it but knocked it off onto the floor. It continued to ring. Swearing softly to himself, he slid off the bed, dragging sheets and blankets with him and landed on top of the phone. He picked it up and looked at the caller ID. It was Emily.

"Mornin'," he said in a muffled voice. His head hurt like nothing he'd ever experienced.

"Dad, it's ten o'clock. You sound like I just woke you up. Are you still in bed? Are you sick?"

Henry's foggy remembrance of the previous night led him to believe he was under questioning again. "I'm not sure about anything," he mumbled.

"Maybe I should come over."

"No, but thanks. I'll get in the shower. I'll be fine." His head cleared. *Did she just call me Dad a second ago?*

After a few moments silence, she said, "Byron's trying to make up for the vase throwing the other night and has rented a small house at Folly Beach for a few days. He wants me to join him and…" She stopped.

Henry sat up on the floor, leaning back against the bed to try to clear his head. *Is she asking for advice from me?* he wondered. Maybe for the first time since…high school? Taking a leap, he said, "And you're not sure what to do?"

"Yes."

After last night, Henry was not much in a trusting mood anymore for people he didn't know. And he already disliked Byron. Emily must still have feelings for him or she wouldn't be hesitating. And she's in grad school, not high school. "Are you somewhat uneasy, or possibly scared, of being alone with him now?"

"Yes, maybe so. I…" she trailed off.

"If you go, do you want me to stop by this afternoon and see how things are going?"

"Yes, I'd like that."

"Text me the address and keep me posted."

"Thanks, Dad."

He sat and thought about what he had just volunteered to do. He wasn't sure he could stand up, much less confront Byron if needed. First, though, I need a cold shower and some coffee. My God, I was tested mentally last night over Palmer, and now I might have to face a test with Byron later today. His investigation appeared to be reaching a level of intensity he had not expected.

Henry dragged himself up, headed for the shower. Passing the mirror, he stopped and looked. He wondered if he still looked like a clown. He thought not, but last night showed how he could be taken in by strangers after drinking in excess, and almost talk himself into a deep hole by a lady with her hand on his knee. He had surprised himself by the way he extricated himself from the conversation. He didn't remember what he said exactly, but it felt good at the time and put a halt to the interrogation by Janice.

Thinking on it, it was quite a performance by those characters in order to…what? How did they know I'd been at the airport and talked to Sam as Charlie before going to Palmer's office as Charles? He didn't think it was Sam, and the only other person close enough to hear the conversation was the boy cleaning the floor. Could he be working for Palmer just to pick up on any conversations that might relate to Palmer in some way? And especially someone acting like Charlie, saying he was going to just walk in Palmer's office and ask for a ride on his jet. Palmer didn't get the word on "Charlie" until after "Charles" had come to visit.

It sure didn't take Palmer long to find him and put a production together of two men and three women to find out what Charlie was sniffing around for. Was it about drugs? Was it about Martha? Or both? In a few more minutes, Janice could have found the answers. Henry now remembered what he said to Janice that ended the conversation. A sick feeling formed in the pit of his stomach. Now what will they do? I'm no match for Palmer and Pedro.

Leaning on the vanity top, still looking in the mirror, it occurred to him for the first time, that last night he had wandered into a trap set by Palmer to find out how much he knew. And now they know "airport" Charlie was "three-piece suit" Charles. His eyes widened as his eyebrows shot up. He exhaled through pursed lips. This thought brought him to attention and swept away most of his hangover, which had now become the least of his worries.

———

In midafternoon, Henry drove out to Folly Beach and found the house where Emily was meeting Byron. It was one of the few remaining "old" beach houses on Folly that hadn't been torn down and turned into a multistory McMansion. The weathered gray siding enclosed one floor with two bedrooms and an open area for cooking, eating, and relaxing. Set ten feet off the ground on timber piling, small porches and front and rear with steps leading down to the sand, completed the picture.

Emily had texted two hours earlier that she had just arrived, and that Byron was opening a bottle of champagne. This would allow her time to see how things developed. Henry parked a block down the street and walked to the house where he saw Emily's white SUV and Byron's black Hummer. It was a warm day, not hot enough for air conditioning. He could hear music coming through the screen doors. Having met Byron as Charlie weeks ago in the hotel lounge with Britt, he was dressed in casual clothes and would be Emily's father today. He decided to wait outside under the house until he heard any arguing. He figured Byron would be getting loud before long.

It wasn't ten minutes before he heard him yelling. Henry eased up the front stairs, staying below the porch enough so he could just see into the house. Emily and Byron were toward the back, standing in front of the kitchen counter with two champagne bottles sitting on top. Byron had a glass in his hand; he was pointing at her as he talked. Emily's glass was on the counter as she leaned against it.

"Something I need to ask you," said Byron, "I saw you with some guy in a restaurant last week. You appeared to be having a big time, smiling and laughing at everything he said. What's up with all that? Are you seeing him now?"

"I went out to dinner with him once. That's all. He happened to be a nice guy and made me laugh. I needed a good laugh."

"I don't understand anymore what it takes to make you happy."

"Your comments about my mother are not laughing matters. You continually bring her up and how she, according to you, all but drove me to suicide with her criticism of everything I did. And you were upset over her not approving of you, saying you weren't good enough for me. I'm beginning to think she was right about you. I'm fucking tired of you still whining about her."

"Well, I'm glad she's not around anymore, but it feels like you've stepped right into her shoes the way you act these days. Now you criticize me over any little thing."

"Oh, Byron, you poor, misunderstood forty-year-old. We need to find a nanny for you. And, by the way, where were *you* that night she drowned in her car?"

"None of your fucking business!" he screamed. "You're just like her, and one day *you'll* end up in the river!"

Emily stepped over and slapped him hard in the face, sending him reeling backward.

Henry was up and running through the door. He saw Byron, his face red, clench his fists and take a step toward Emily, who was reaching for one of the champagne bottles.

"Don't you dare touch her," yelled Henry as he ran toward them.

Byron turned and looked back at him.

"Who the hell are you?" he yelled.

Henry barreled into him just as Emily swung a bottle that grazed his head but cracked into his shoulder with a thud. Byron hit the floor, out cold, with Henry on top of him.

Bent over Henry, Emily helped him up.

"Jesus, is that you, Dad?" she asked. "Where'd you come from? How'd you do that?"

Henry stood, dazed.

Emily hugged him. "Thank you. Thank you for being here."

Henry looked down.

"You'd better call 911 and get EMS over here." He knelt down and felt for a pulse. "He's okay, but he'll have a headache." He stood and took the bottle from her hands and set it on the counter.

"I don't recognize you anymore," she said. "Now you're a commando." She looked down at Byron. "What an ass he is." Looking back up, she squeezed his hands. "I brought some wine. How about a glass?"

"Excellent, I think I could use a sip. You know, what I did just now scared me to death."

Henry stared at Emily for a moment. "What would Martha have thought of what I just did?"

"I think she would have been very proud of you."

The stirring of Byron still laying at their feet, along with the sound of a siren approaching, brought their conversation to a halt.

# CHAPTER 22

Henry made his way over to Britt's place early in the evening after that afternoon's encounter with Byron. His head was still foggy from the previous evening with Janice, and his body hurt from this morning's encounter with Byron. But he knew he must lay out what happened while the details were still fresh in his mind.

Britt met him at the door. "You look like hell, Henry. What happened?"

"I feel worse than I look. I've been stretched to my limits mentally and physically over the last two days. Quite a sequence of events. Have you got a few minutes?"

"Of course, I do. Come in and sit down. I'll get us something."

"I'll just take some water, please. And do you happen to have anything that might kick back this headache I have?"

"Yes, I do," she said from the kitchen. "There's some Advil in the medicine cabinet over the sink in the bathroom, or maybe the drawer beside the sink."

Henry shuffled off to the bathroom. Opening the drawer, he didn't see the Advil, but he did notice a pair of glasses with a broken chain. He looked in the medicine cabinet and spotted the Advil. He noticed a prescription bottle next to the Advil labeled belladonna phenobarbital. That's interesting, he thought, taking three Advil from the bottle and heading back to couch.

Britt walked in with a glass of wine and a glass of water for him.

"Britt, I couldn't help but notice the bottle of medicine in your cabinet called belladonna phenobarbital. I didn't know belladonna was still used in the medical profession."

"Sure is. It's used for stomach ulcers in some cases. Recently, I developed stomach ulcers, and my doctor prescribed it for me. It seems to help."

"It's a wonder with all of us in the English lit profession, I didn't need it too. I guess my cognac took care of me." He smiled to himself, sitting back to try to organize his thoughts.

"Well, Henry, tell me what you got yourself into the last couple of days."

He leaned forward, a look of exhaustion in his eyes.

"It began yesterday morning when I took that mechanic you found for me to the salvage yard to help me search Martha's car again. We found Jack's handkerchief in the car…the same one he used to wipe the rain off his face when he walked in the restaurant! A light blue silk one with his initials sewn on it. We had to take the seat out to find it stuck in the webbing under the bottom of the seat. How it could end up there, I have no idea. But there it was. He was in her car that night!" Henry stopped, out of breath. He took a slow sip of his water.

He started in again. "I *knew* she was too smart to just drive into the water…even with the storm and the lights out. I *knew* it was Jack, and now I have the proof."

"Well," she said in a quiet voice, "what are you going to do now?"

Henry slumped back and looked up to the ceiling.

"I don't know." He looked back down at his water, picked it up, and swirled it around. Still looking at his glass, he said, "You'd think I'd know. But I don't." His excitement ebbed, causing his shoulders to slump. "I guess I never figured I'd get this far."

"I don't know what to say, Henry, but you don't have to figure it out tonight."

His eyes lit up, and he straightened himself.

"But that's not all that happened yesterday."

He told her about going to The English Club to celebrate and the two men who joined him. And then they all went on to Henry's, where he knew he was way over his intake of alcohol limit. "And three women joined the party." Janice had slid in next to him, with her hand on his thigh, questioning him about his trip to Palmer's office.

"She knew that I was Charlie at the airport and Charles in front of Palmer. But I was Henry at the beginning of my chat with Janice, and she was calling me Charlie by the end of her interrogation. Maybe I like being Charlie more than Henry." He chuckled. "Now that I think about it, I've acquired most of my information from various people being Charlie the tourist."

"So, someone at the airport must have tipped off Palmer right after you saw him."

"I would guess it was the guy sweeping the floor. Sam wouldn't do it, and the girl at the desk was too far away to hear anything. Palmer didn't have the Charlie and Charles connection when I was in front of him. But he had it shortly thereafter, and in time to set up the Janice rendezvous a few days later. He must have discovered that I went to the English pub, which means he's had his eyes on me for some time. But why? And all Janice got out of me was confirmation that Charlie was Charles and was really Henry."

"That's quite a story, Charlie. Right out of the movies."

"Well, what do you think of all this interest in me by Palmer?"

"This is a tough one," said Britt. "We've kidded around about Pedro and drug money, but never thought it could actually be true. They have something going on that they don't want you to know about, and they might be scared about what you might already know. The question is…is it about Martha's death or possible drug money? Or both. Or something we don't even know about?"

"You've been around Palmer for years and know Rita. Is there anything you can think of that is a little strange, over the top, or out of sync with what you would consider normal behavior for people of their status and position?"

"Off the top of my head, one thing is that Rita is known for always paying cash for most everything she buys. Groceries, restaurant bills, everyday things. I only know this because other people have asked her why she does this. Apparently, growing up in Puerto Rico, her family was very poor, and she remembers her parents not always able to buy everyday things for their family. She pays cash for these items to remind her how lucky she is to be able to do so…and to not forget her parents' struggle."

"That's kind of strange, but it makes sense in a way," said Henry, thinking on it. "On a devious level, I guess it might also be a way to launder money, little by little."

"That might be a reach, but I don't know anything about laundering money," said Britt. "But come to think of it, I remember Palmer telling me one night after an extra-long cocktail hour that Rita's father helped them out with a monthly cash stipend to help maintain his and Rita's status in Charleston society. Rita had told him of Palmer's consistent bad luck with his sports gambling, which created quite a backlash with threats of a divorce at the time. Her father finally accepted the situation, knowing Palmer would never stop his gambling."

"I guess the Middletons being patrons of the arts and theater is normal fare for old time Charleston families?"

"Yes, it is. You're seldom sure where the 'old money' came from, only that it's there. But it's known Rita's father had turned his life around, as evident in the hotels he now owns along with the jet parked over at the airport. Word is import-export business and real estate, which means it could come from anywhere. So, I don't see anything on the surface that can't be explained away."

"I'm confused right now. This afternoon, I stopped Byron from attacking Emily because she asked him what he was doing on the night Martha drowned. Yesterday morning, I found evidence Jack was in her car that night. Then, when I was celebrating yesterday afternoon, I found myself being interrogated by Palmer's people, as if they had something to hide. I now have three possible suspects who might have a reason to kill Martha.

Is this called making headway in an investigation?"

"Yes, it's all part of the process. You'll sort it all out. You're smart enough and tenacious enough to figure this out."

"Thank you for saying that. You don't realize how much I've come to depend on you to keep me on track." He shook his head. "And now I must confront Jack," he whispered.

# CHAPTER 23

Henry was confused. He had evidence of Jack being in the car with his handkerchief, but Jack's retelling of how she died the last time they had talked didn't offer any clues that he was involved. Henry decided that he had to confront Jack about the handkerchief and see his reaction to being accused of murder. Henry was still wary of Jack, even though he had trained to protect himself.

He dressed in his casual clothes and went to Jack's favorite bar. He sat at the end of the bar, saving a seat for Jack.

Jack arrived and sat down.

"Glad to see football is back," said Henry, looking up at the TV.

"So am I," said Jack as he turned his attention to the bartender. He ordered the usual.

His head down, Henry said, "You're Jack Townsend, I believe, and if you don't mind, I'd like to ask you a question."

"Fire away, Henry."

Henry's head snapped around. He almost knocked over his beer.

"Thought so," said Jack, staring at Henry. "What's on your mind?"

"How did you know?"

"Oh, I thought about the excuse you used last time you were in here, when I called you on using the word 'acquired'." He took a pull on his drink. "It was damn convincing at the time, but I got sidetracked with that guy at the table behind us and had to leave. But it came back to me later. Acquired. No one ever uses a word like that in any context, except maybe a lawyer. It's not in a normal person's vocabulary. Certainly not Charlie's, no matter what the story he came up with on the fly. At the time, I didn't see chubby Professor Henry Willis in Charlie, but now I do. So, Henry Willis, what's on your mind?"

Henry was dumbfounded, speechless, and now on the defensive. So, he started at the top.

"I just found your blue handkerchief, with your initials on it, in Martha's car after she drowned. You were the only one who was there that night, could see her leave alone to the garage, and were mad at her for telling you to leave forever. You had the motive and the opportunity."

"And?"

"You followed her to the car, somehow got her to the boat ramp, into the water, and let her drown."

"You're partially correct."

"What do you mean?"

"After I left the restaurant, I cooled off in the rain and followed her to the car to talk to her. In the restaurant, she had told me the fairy tale was over and to never contact her again. I needed to tell her that I was no longer obsessed with her, even though I flirted with her in front of you at the restaurant. When I saw her that evening as I was walking by the restaurant, I just had to come in and say what had been on my mind all those years to make her feel good…and to make you mad."

"Well, what's with all the antics and storming out when Martha told you to go away forever."

"Something clicks in me when someone, anyone, tries to give me an order. I usually get in a fight. But for Martha, I just walked away. I wasn't mad at her."

"Why the handkerchief?"

"I told her I had spotted someone new, someone younger, who had taken her place, and I was just having fun flattering her in front of you. She said she had believed all those things I had said in the restaurant, and now it was all a lie. I told her I wasn't lying, it's that I had seen a younger *version* of her. Her eyes began to tear up, so I handed her my handkerchief, said goodbye, got out of her car, and walked out of the parking garage. I didn't know anything had happened until I was contacted by the police the next day. I told them that after leaving her in the garage, I walked to the bar we're in right now for a drink. As I walked in, the lights went out from the power outages. I had a drink and paid in cash as the power was still off. The regular bartender was not there, and the fill-in didn't recognize or remember me. Then I walked straight to my place. So, nobody saw me after I left Martha, and I couldn't prove I was in this bar."

In silence, Henry stared at him. He believed Jack. It was a convincing story. Martha *had* reveled in his flattery and soaked it up until she had to send him away. She was going away with Henry, and it was time to call a halt to everything. And maybe with the extra wine coupled with little food, any glow that she felt for the nice words was punctured when he revealed that he had spotted a younger version of her.

Henry was crushed to learn all this. First, the man he had thought all along was Martha's killer was apparently not. And Martha reveled in his inane flattery to the point that she all but cried when he told her it was for somebody else. If what Jack said was the truth, and right now he believed it was, he was seeing a part of Jack and a part of Martha that he never understood.

"Did you see anyone else in the garage when you were there?" asked Henry.

"There were a few cars leaving, but I didn't see anyone on foot…although I wasn't particularly keeping a lookout for anyone."

"I must ask you something. Why did you follow her all those years, even after being married and having a son?"

"Simple, Henry. I loved her."

Henry tried to absorb what he had just been told. Jack had been obsessed with Martha for decades. Even with his hair-trigger temper, Henry believed Jack would not suddenly decide to kill Martha. Jack could get in a bar fight easily enough, but to suddenly kill a person he has loved for all those years? His knee-jerk reaction that Jack was guilty may have been wrong. There was nothing to say. He took a twenty-dollar bill from his wallet, lay it on the bar, and looked at Jack.

"I have to go," he said in a quiet voice before walking away.

———

Henry pushed through the bar door and into the heat of the city and became dizzy under the glare of the low sun. The sidewalk was crowded with people, and Henry had difficulty maintaining his balance as he tried to evade bumping into people. The thought that Jack may not be the killer deflated him, confused him. All of his thoughts, all of his anger, and all of his work to become a "new Henry" had been directed at Jack Townsend. For months, he had pushed aside other possible suspects to second place in favor of Jack. He was the obvious one. With his quick temper, he had the motive, had the opportunity, and his handkerchief was in the car. And yet, Henry believed the man's explanation of what happened that night. He thought of how Jack described his new love was a younger version of Martha. Could it be he was talking of Emily? His legs almost buckled at the thought.

Stepping into a shaded doorway, he called Emily and asked her if he could buy her a drink.

———

They met at a quiet bistro on a side street where they could talk. Henry told her of his meeting with Jack a few hours earlier and his explanation of what happened that night and that he had found a younger version of Martha.

"Has Jack Townsend approached you in any way?" asked Henry.

"Funny you should ask," she said, a smile crossing her face. "I picked him up about a week back and got him to buy me dinner."

"Huh? You what?"

"Thought I might cozy up to him a bit and see if I could find out any information from him for you."

Henry shook his head in disbelief. Only Emily would do such a thing. "Did you give him your real name?"

"Sure did. Didn't mention to him that you were in town."

"I can't believe it. What did he say?"

"He said he had heard about the drowning and gave me his condolences. I asked him if he'd ever heard of someone drowning like that. He said no, but he knew where that boat ramp was because he launches his fishing boat from there. He said they have cross bars there now, so that no one can drive into the river by mistake again. He was very casual about it, and the conversation moved on to sports and flying. He's quite the character."

"Would you believe him? I mean, if he told you what he told me?"

"I believe I would, although I only spent a little over an hour with him. He's not the flashy type like Byron, who can spew out a lot of drivel trying to make an impression. Jack comes across like an excited little boy when he gets started on some of his stories. But he must have a serious, intelligent side, if he flies jet airplanes for a living. I will say, though, when he asked about my background, I learned he doesn't know the slightest thing about English literature or any of the arts."

"Then what did you talk about? You're not exactly up to speed on sports or airplanes."

"I don't know exactly but the time passed quickly. It was refreshing to talk to someone not caught up on college of the arts or law school." She looked off in thought. "I'll be seeing him again, I know that."

"In that case, I should mention something I learned about Jack a few weeks ago that I think you should know," said Henry. He then went on to recount Jack's actions at the sports lounge, when Jack confronted the guy who was laughing at him as his date whispered in his ear. He also shared Britt's subsequent explanation of Jack's insecurity of his manhood, as Patrick was gay. "So, it appears that Patrick hadn't been tailing you, but tailing Byron, who, according to Britt, 'has been known to have boyfriends from time to time.'"

Emily was speechless. She shook her head. "My God. Nothing is as it seems or what you thought it was. Everyone and everything connected with Martha in any way has another story hidden beneath the surface."

# CHAPTER 24

For Henry, everything was turning upside down. It was becoming apparent that neither Jack nor Martha were who they appeared to be. In some respects, they were the antithesis of who he thought they were.

The next day, Henry called Britt, asking if he might stop by for a talk. She agreed, asking if he would come for dinner. Henry arrived at her door with a fine bottle of cabernet in hand.

The door opened, and Britt stood in a white cotton summer dress, a rope belt around her waist, her blond hair tied back at the nape of her neck, her blue eyes sparkling.

"My, are you looking fine tonight," said Henry. "You look ready for a photo shoot."

She smiled. "I thought you might like this." She shook her head as if embarrassed. "I just like dressing up a bit now and then."

He handed her the bottle, following her as she headed for the kitchen. Sounds of contemporary jazz filtered softly from hidden speakers. He sat perched on the stool at the kitchen bar and gazed at her exposed shoulders, her tan highlighted by her white filmy blouse. She stood across from him at the stove, stirring the pot in slow careful circles with a wooden spoon. They had not spoken for some minutes. Only the soft jazz playing intruded on the silence as he sipped his wine and debated what he should say, if anything. For months, she had helped him navigate the new world into which he had stepped. She always acted as a friend, in a professional manner, and that had not changed. But he had. She always made dinner for him weekly to kick around ideas in a more relaxed atmosphere. Tonight, he had to tell her. He had to say it. Feeling his heart against his chest, he took a deep breath.

Before he could speak, she turned around with a smile.

"We should be ready to eat in just a few minutes. I have beef bourguignon bubbling in a pot that should go well with the red wine you brought."

The moment was lost for Henry. He just nodded.

"Well," she said, "it sounded like you have some important news to share with me. I'm hoping it's good news?"

"I wouldn't say it was good news, but I had a very interesting talk with Jack Townsend, as Henry, the other afternoon at the sports lounge."

"You what? You talked with him as Henry, not Charlie?"

"After I found his handkerchief in Martha's car, I figured it was time to ask him how it came to be in her car."

"Did you introduce yourself to kick things off?"

"I didn't have to. He had already guessed that Charlie was actually Henry. I'd made the mistake of using the word 'acquired' in a sentence a few weeks back, something Charlie would never do. Jack had berated me in times past for using, what he thought, were fancy words."

"What did he have to say about the handkerchief?"

"He said that he followed Martha to the garage and sat in the car with her for a few moments. He said she began crying when he told her he had spotted someone to take her place, someone who was a younger version of her. He gave her his handkerchief, got out, and walked away."

"Those are tough words to put on a lady my age." She sipped her wine for a moment. "You know, I don't think Jack killed her. He's hot tempered with other men, but all I've ever seen or heard about him from other women is that he's a pussycat around them. He guards, projects his manhood with men, but with women he becomes anxious, almost intimidated."

"I asked why he followed her all these years. 'Simple,' he said, 'I loved her'."

"Do you believe him?"

"I think I do." He stopped, looking off. "I talked with Emily last evening after seeing Jack, and she told me she 'picked him up' and went to dinner with him last week. She told him who she was, but not about me being in town. Emily said she was trying to find information on him that might be of help to me. It scared me to hear this, but isn't it just like Emily to step over the line? She didn't learn anything, although she said it was a fun evening." He shook his head. "I believe she's thinking of seeing him again."

Britt's face changed, as if she were contemplating a serious question. She leaned on the counter and took Henry by the hands.

"Henry, I've got to tell you something that I'm ashamed I was part of. And I'm sorry that it will hurt you, but under the present circumstances, and now that Jack has had dinner with Emily, and who knows where this will go, I've got to tell you this."

She took a deep breath, looked into his eyes, and said, "Martha had an ongoing affair with Jack that began about five years ago…soon after Phillip died. I think it was a reflex action on her part for, as she put it, you 'dragging your heels' until it was too late to make the drive to see Phillip that night. So, she would see Jack when she came down here three or four times a year on the pretense of going to a convention, special speaking engagement, or whatever. They would drive around in his car, with the top down, and have dinner together. I've thought about this a lot. I think their affair was like a marriage for Jack. It gave him some emotional stability, yet it allowed him to act like a college student when Martha was not in town. For Martha, it was the reverse. She had emotional stability with you and could act like a college student with Jack. It might have been a perfect world for them both. To me, it seems it's like he never grew up. He's still in college in some ways. It may be that he got hurt by someone he really liked and has never gotten over it. He may have loved Martha, yet he also realized she'd never leave you."

Speechless, Henry's mouth dropped open, his eyes wide. How is this possible? Martha and Jack? The fucking jet jockey? He stood and slapped his hands hard on the countertop. "Tell me you made this up, Britt. A grand joke because Jack told me he loved her. Right?"

She stood motionless, silent, with tears appearing in her eyes. Just above a whisper, she said, "I'm sorry to say I helped coordinate and enable the deception. She had a separate credit card under my address here. She asked me to keep all the receipts for tax write-offs, knowing you never looked at the tax returns. I have most of the receipts."

He gave her a disbelieving look that gradually turned to shock. She progressed with the story before fading into a look of despair by the end. He sat down.

"No, it can't be. Martha? And Jack?" He felt the blood drain out of his face. His head dropped to his arms laying on the counter. "My God, how can this be? If this is true, I never knew the *real* Martha. She cheated on me for five years? With Jack? It's a wonder he didn't laugh in my face yesterday." He stopped, a furrow in his brow. "He told Martha he had spotted a younger version of her. And then Emily was nice enough to invite herself out with him last week. Jesus." He shook his head. "May I see the receipts?"

She went to her bedroom and came out carrying two shoeboxes. She set them on the counter, as if they were fragile, and stepped back to lean against the counter, her arms wrapped around her chest.

He opened the first box and began to look at the credit card statements and receipts. Tears welled in his eyes as he studied the bits of paper that traced a path through bars, restaurants, gifts—on and on. He opened the other box and shuffled through more of the same. He shook his head, wiped his eyes, and put the lids on both the boxes. He then swept them off the counter and onto the floor where they exploded, receipts flying everywhere.

He picked up his glass of wine, stopped, then set it back gently on the counter in front of him. "Britt, I'm alone in a sinking boat, and I don't know what to do."

"You're not alone, Henry. You have Emily. You have me and all your friends. We can help you." She reached over to squeeze his hand.

"You really think so? What do I have left? My wife is dead, and I just found out she cheated on me for five years. And the man she had the affair with, and who I thought killed her, is dating our daughter. But that's not all. Then there's Palmer Middleton, who may have a contract out on my head—that is, if Byron doesn't get to me first. And, of all people, I may have to hire Jack to protect me. Fuck!" He looked up.

"Let me serve up some hot dinner and we'll sit down and try not to solve everything in the next five minutes. How's that sound?"

"I'm afraid I won't be much company for dinner tonight. Let's try it another time. I'd like that."

As he stood, she came over and gave him a hug. "Henry, I am so sorry. I can't imagine how much this hurts." She walked with him to the door. "Please call me…for anything." She hugged him again and he shuffled off into the twilight where he found a light rain falling.

Oblivious of the rain, he found his car and began driving slowly, not sure of where he was going, and was startled to see a sign that read Boat Ramp Ahead on Right. He continued on until he came to a stop at the traffic light at the entrance, turned in slowly, and stopped in front of the new gate. He turned off the car, got out, and trudged down the ramp toward the water and floating dock. He walked out to the end of the dock, took his shoes off, sat down, and dropped his bare feet in the warm water. The pungent smell of the marshes and salt water enveloped him. The tide was slack with a few marsh reeds floating by that gave a hint that the tide was about to turn toward the harbor, where it would pass out through the jetties and join the Atlantic. There was no breeze, and the early evening heat draped over him. He felt the beads of rain as they trickled from his forehead down his checks and beneath his shirt collar. Tears that had been gathering in his eyes for months finally fell to his face and joined the beads of water. A bloated fish floated by in the gathering darkness to remind him that he was not alone.

He pulled his legs up, set his heels on the edge of the dock, wrapped his arms around his legs, lowered his head to his knees, and wept.

———

Back in his apartment, Henry fell face down on his bed. He found it hard to imagine Martha and Jack hooking up for weekend trysts every time she was in town for five years. Then she would come home and lay beside him, telling him about how exhausting the meeting or conference had been. He was ashamed he never picked up on this. She must have worked hard not to have slipped up somewhere along the line. But Martha was never one to get surprised at anything. She was always two steps ahead of everybody. He didn't know who he should be angrier at, Martha or Jack. But Martha was the one cheating, not Jack. And Martha was a stronger personality than Jack. Henry was sure she was in charge of that whole operation. And the way she played me months ago at the restaurant when Jack showed up, acting as if she hadn't seen him in thirty years. Henry wished he'd never come on this fishing trip to Charleston. He second-guessed himself on all that he had done since coming to town and had yet to learn who, if anyone, had killed Martha.

# CHAPTER 25

The morning sun rose above the city, pouring through Henry's window and onto his sleeping face. He stirred, trying to escape the nightmare that had chased him for most of the night. He still remembered it clearly: Martha and Jack having dinner together at the Chez Toulouse, sitting at their table, and laughing hilariously as they talked. Henry couldn't hear what they were saying but had a feeling that they were talking about him. He knew they were talking about him. God damn them, he thought. He rolled out and sat on the edge of the bed, staring down at the wood floor. No, it was my fault. I all but bailed out on my family after Phillip's death. He felt responsible, further crawling into his cocoon. He had spurned advice from Martha to get therapy and, in effect, had all but retired to his study. No wonder I lost connection with my wife and daughter. And now I've lost Martha, and Emily could be following in her mother's footsteps with Jack Townsend. Jesus, he doesn't go away.

Henry made coffee and grabbed a stale doughnut from the fridge, considering whether he should tell Emily of her mother's affair with Jack. She should know, shouldn't she? But he was embarrassed that Martha had done this to him, and he had had no clue. He felt ashamed that he had not been more attentive to her. It was humiliating to him, and he was not sure how Emily would react. It was another eye-opening chapter in the underground world that Martha had stepped into from time to time.

———

Henry went to Emily's apartment in the afternoon and told her of finding Jack's handkerchief in Martha's car, and then meeting with Jack. He explained that Jack had spotted a younger version of her and Martha had begun to cry, so he handed her his handkerchief and walked away. Henry then told her of Britt's confession to enabling an affair between Martha and Jack over the last five years.

"I thought you should know, as it appears you'll be seeing more of Jack." He thought she would be disappointed or angry at her mother's affair.

But she only smiled. "So, I finally bested her at something," she said.

At first, her response surprised Henry. Instead of consoling him for being cheated on, she wasn't surprised by her mother's actions. Maybe she understood who Martha was, or could be, better than me. He had had his head in the sand deeper than he first imagined.

"It sounds as if your relationship with Martha was more a contest than a normal mother-daughter conflict."

"It was always difficult to measure up to the standards she thought I should aspire to. The standards she set for me were never within my reach, and if I got close, she'd move them a little higher. So, I retaliated sometimes by going in a different direction altogether. Taking three years off instead of staying in school. Going to law school instead of going for a masters in English. Big enough changes to get her attention. I'm not sure she ever reconciled in her own mind why I did some of these things."

"You don't know how good it makes me feel to finally talk to you. I must apologize again for my lack of attention to you for so many years. I think I lost my ability to connect…as though I subconsciously feared getting too close to someone for fear I'd hurt them in some way. I overcompensated for the anger I had early in my life and became hesitant in the living of the rest of my life. I now believe that I'm finding equilibrium between those two extremes."

Emily reached over and took his hand.

"Dad, I'm so proud of you for just being down here, trying to solve Mom's death. I would never have thought you had it in you to do such a thing."

"Well, I've got to go back to the beginning, now that Jack appears no longer to be *the* guilty one. Maybe I missed something by being obsessed with Jack? What about all those other people without alibis? Where was Byron, if not with you? Palmer was most likely at the retirement ceremony, but he sure as hell didn't do it; his men may have, though. Britt and George were sort of together, but neither had an alibi. Where were they? I saw you with Byron for a while, but you and he must have split up since he didn't have an alibi."

"I don't know where he went. He'd been chatting up the ladies all afternoon, and I was tired of it, so when you and Mom left, I went straight to my place by myself and cooked dinner."

"Did Byron ever mention what he told the police when they questioned him?"

"He was tight lipped about it. Said he went straight home. I think he struck out with the ladies and was embarrassed about it." Emily smiled. "Byron, the Mad Hatter. He's sure explosive enough to possibly do such a thing, but he doesn't strike me as someone who would plan such an intricate killing. He would have hit her on the head with a bottle and ran."

"So, it's just his word?" said Henry.

"Yes, that's it."

"Did you ever hear from George or Britt and what they did?"

"No, by the time the police had gone around questioning people, everyone had scattered. Asking them now would almost feel like you were accusing them."

"You might be right, but at this point, being the widower of Martha, I will assume the mantle of an official investigator. I'll figure out a way to ask the questions without offending anybody." He stopped. "You know it would seem that George and Britt would have gone to dinner together after the official dinner shrunk to only those wanting to remain. It was George's first trip to Charleston in almost a year, and they always got together and talked 'theater.' Let's call him. He doesn't know about Jack yet either. I'll put him on speaker and let him know you and I are trying to look at the investigation with new eyes."

Henry called George in Asheville and brought him up to date on all the latest developments: his meeting with Palmer, the incident with Janice, and Jack's presumed innocence.

"What a turn of events, Henry," said George. "It's hard to believe that Palmer may somehow be mixed up in all this, but your talk with him… and later this Janice, sure looks like he has something to hide. So, where do you go from here?"

"I'm trying to place where everyone was the night Martha died, in case they may have seen or heard something that might be a clue to what really happened. You probably already told me this, but did you and Britt go to dinner with anyone else that night?"

"We never went to dinner. Britt had told me earlier she wasn't feeling well, and when the news of your one-night dalliance surfaced, she begged off dinner, saying she wouldn't be very good company. I finished off the hors d'oeuvres at the party and went to my room. So, I didn't really see anyone else until you called saying Martha was missing and we all geared up to search."

"Yes, I remember you telling me all this now. I'm afraid my brain has been over stimulated from all of the revelations I've been bombarded with on Martha, Jack, and everything I've come in contact with since coming to town. Quite the opposite from walking down the tree-lined sidewalk every morning to Allen Hall to give another lecture on English lit."

"I can only imagine, Henry."

Henry hung up and looked at Emily. "It seems nobody has an airtight alibi." He shook his head. "And I'm *assuming* that my lead suspect is telling me the truth. Martha's rebuttal of him at the restaurant might have clicked that hot button of his. I'm back to motive and opportunity, and it's hard to argue that he couldn't have known what a handful Martha could be when she got her back up. I'm sure Jack could well imagine what she would be like when she found out he was after you. Maybe we should talk to him again and see if we can learn anything new."

"I'll call him," said Emily, "and see if he can stop by this afternoon or in the morning."

# CHAPTER 26

An hour later, Jack rang the doorbell and stuck his head in.

"Come on in, Jack" said Emily, "sit down and have a beer with us, if you want."

"No thanks on the beer. What's on your mind?" he asked as he walked in and took a seat.

"Thanks for stopping by," said Henry. "I have some questions about the night Martha died that you may be able to help us with. As you probably know, Emily had been seeing Byron. And some weeks back, Emily called me and said your son, Patrick, was following her. This prompted me to come straight down here and find out what was going on. It seemed she only spotted Patrick when she was out at a restaurant or lounge with Byron. I guess I have to ask if you knew about this?"

"I first spotted Emily at a restaurant about a month before Martha died, but had no idea who she was," claimed Jack. "Then I saw her with you at Martha's funeral and later as she was leaving your house. I learned her name from the church handout. I followed her to Charleston but lost her in the city. I found where she lived and had Patrick follow her for a few weeks or so. He saw she was seeing a man we later learned was Byron, from the college. After that, we didn't follow her, so you must be mistaken about seeing Patrick a couple months after the funeral."

"Jack," said Henry, "I was concerned about Byron's attitude toward Martha, and I followed him and Emily to a restaurant a couple of weeks ago. When a young man sat down not far from their table, Emily signaled me that it was Patrick. When Emily and Byron left the restaurant in the middle of a fight, I went out the door after them and bumped into the young man she had pointed out. I asked him why he was following them. All he said was, 'My name is Patrick.' I ran on to catch up behind Emily and Byron. Do you have any idea why Patrick would still be tailing Emily?"

Jack sat stone faced, saying nothing.

Emily spoke up.

"Jack, would it be okay if I explained something we have learned just recently about Byron that might help clarify our question about Patrick?"

Jack stared at her a moment before nodding.

"It seems that Byron, although he usually dates women, from time to time has been known to have boyfriends. We believe now that Patrick may have been tailing Byron, not me.

This is of no consequence to us either way than simply explaining why Patrick continued to appear to be tailing me. All we're interested in is finding out whether Mom was killed by someone. We believe that it was not an accident, and Byron's repeated slamming of Martha's treatment of me and his volatile temper, led us to wonder if he could have carried his words a step further against my mother. He doesn't have an alibi, other than he went directly home…not unlike what you told the police other than stopping by the sports lounge. Henry saw his black Hummer in the parking garage that night, still parked almost an hour after Martha left the restaurant."

"Where are you going with all of this?"

"Well," said Emily, "recently, I politely asked Byron if he went straight home after the party that evening and this set him off. It ended in a fight, where he tried to hit me with a bottle of champagne." She looked over at Henry. "Dad showed up just in time, tackled him, and knocked him out." She smiled at him, then turned back at Jack. "I have not seen him, nor do

I want to see him again. We're still curious about Byron's whereabouts that evening, and wonder if Patrick could give us any lead as to where Byron might have been between about 6:00 and 8:00 p.m. that evening?"

"And why do you think Patrick might know?" said Jack, his voice rising.

Her voice steady, Emily replied, "We asked all the women at the party if they had seen Byron after the party or knew of anyone who did or might know. None of them had seen him afterward. Some remember him leaving by himself, somewhat upset and…"

Jack interrupted. "And since Patrick is gay, maybe they met up?"

"Yes," said Emily.

Jack stood and walked to the window, looking out for a moment. Turning back and facing them, he said, "Patrick lived in San Francisco for the last ten years, and when he showed up here four months ago, it was the first time I'd seen him in those ten years. I was ashamed of him all those years and distanced myself from him. And now, I'm ashamed of myself for doing that."

He walked back and sat down. "To answer your question, yes. Patrick and Byron met up that evening. When I was in the sports lounge after leaving Martha, I got a call that Patrick was in the emergency room at the hospital. It was Byron who called me. They had had a fight, and Byron said he had hit Patrick and may have broken his nose. I went straight to the hospital and talked to them both. Patrick's nose was bandaged up, I signed him out and took him home. So, you see, all three of us had alibis for that evening. We just didn't want to admit it."

# CHAPTER 27

Henry now faced a very difficult and delicate, but necessary, conversation with Jack. He waited until the next day to approach him. He had to ask Jack about his affair with Martha. He had to know what happened. How did it start? It had been about five years since their son, Phillip, had overdosed. Had her anger and disappointment in Henry's inaction to go to the college that night he overdosed have prompted Martha to accept an invitation from Jack to go out?

He decided to ask Jack to meet him at the sports bar, so if Jack became out of control, there'd be people around. Henry thought a talk concerning an affair shouldn't be discussed sitting at the bar, so he sat in a booth where Jack spotted him and slid in across from him. Henry put a twenty on the table and ordered a beer, while Jack requested his usual bourbon on the rocks.

Jack smiled. "Well, Henry, what's on your mind today?"

Henry had practiced what his opening to Jack would be, but at this moment, it disappeared. He blinked and began the best he could. "Jack, I have to ask you something that makes me very uncomfortable to talk about, and I'm sure it'll be the same for you. But it needs to be spoken about, as you are now dating my daughter. It concerns her mother."

"Okay, what is it?"

Henry took a deep breath and dove in.

"I had a conversation with Britt the other night. She told me that you had an affair with Martha over the last five years or so, when she would come to town alone. Martha had her own credit card with a local address and paid Britt to take care of it. She showed me receipts from restaurants, bars, and so on when Martha paid for anything. Your name is not on the receipts, of course, so I only have Britt's word that you were present for these outings."

Jack looked hard at Henry, his jaw clenched. He said nothing.

Henry continued, his voice quiet.

"You told me a few days ago that you loved her." Henry swallowed and took a moment before he asked, "Did she love you?"

"Yes," he said, "but as a sister loves a brother." He looked off a moment. "We enjoyed each other's company. We had fun just driving around with the top down. She told me it might be fun to drive off into the sunset."

"What the hell does that mean?" said Henry, sitting up straighter.

"I don't know exactly. She laughed when she said it. But we shared stories about ourselves all the time…anything that made us laugh. I could tell her things I wouldn't tell anyone else. I think we could both just be ourselves, knowing there would be no judgment. What we said would go no further than the table where we were sitting. She could just be Martha and not the PhD professor and all the conditions that it brought. And I could just be me and not become nervous trying to impress her with my limited range of interest. She became my best friend, and I became a better person." He took a long pull on his drink.

Henry was caught off guard by Jack's answer, surprised by his perception and use of words. At the moment, he didn't know what to think. He hadn't known what to expect from his question. But Jack's insightful explanation of the "affair," he thought, is too unique to have been made up on the spot. What disturbed him, though, was Martha's apparent comment to Jack that "we'll drive off into the sunset." What the hell did that mean? But at the restaurant months ago, she had told him to go away. Had she changed her mind, or had Jack misinterpreted what she had said? In any case, at the time, I was about to drive off into the sunset with her. Henry did not ask if he slept with her. He didn't think so and didn't want to know. He believed the story as Jack explained it. But he would check on the receipts at Britt's for hotel rooms, although Jack did have a condo.

"Do you believe her death was an accident?" asked Henry.

"I've thought about it a lot. First of all, I don't know of anyone who would have had a reason to kill her. And under those conditions in such an unorthodox method and make it look like an accident? It would be tough to pull off. To answer your question…yes, I believe it was an accident. At night, in the middle of a storm and a blackout in the area, if you weren't paying attention you could drive through that intersection and find yourself driving down that boat ramp before you realized what had happened. Martha was upset when she left the garage and could have easily been distracted after our conversation, her mind wandering long enough to get her in trouble."

"You may be right," said Henry, "but I don't believe it was an accident."

Jack stood. "I have to be going. Thanks for the drink." He turned to go, then spun around. "By the way, I never slept with her." He walked off.

Henry just stared at him as he walked away. Even though this conversation was some consolation to Henry, he slumped in his seat. He was exhausted by…everything. If he had been in the garage with her that night, Jack would not have talked to her, an accident would not have happened, and if a killer had been waiting for her, they would have been scared off. No matter what actually happened, his usual inaction—not unlike that with his son, Phillip—had caused another death in his family. He felt the only way to somewhat temper his guilt would be to avenge her death, because he still believed she had been murdered.

He got up, walked out, and returned to his apartment. Henry sat at his small dining table with a glass of cognac. Tired and deflated, he was no closer to solving his wife's death than the day he first drove into town. Suddenly, he stood up and screamed as loud as he could. He picked up the side of the table and flipped it upside down onto the floor, sending cognac and glasses flying. God! He was so pissed. That should wake up any napping neighbors, he thought. Good.

# CHAPTER 28

Emily checked with a friend of hers who worked at the hospital, confirming that Jack Townsend had signed for the release of Patrick and Byron the night of the storm. That took Jack and Byron off the list, but there remained one suspect who still held his attention. Palmer Middleton had reacted to his visit in less than two days with an intercept involving two men who followed him to the Old English Club and had three women waiting at "Henry's" to finish off the ambush. They had to have been following him around town for some time to have known his favorite secluded oasis. Did the bartender tip off the two guys, who were on standby, who then alerted the three women? He wondered now if he should have played along with Janice to see where they were heading, although he realized now he was probably lucky just to have walked away.

This amount of energy to keep up with all the characters and their actions, and trying to diagnose what they meant in the context of his investigation, was taking a toll on his senses. He felt he had one last effort in him. Palmer Middleton. And it included a special gift for himself, for having survived these past months in Charleston with his body and brain still intact. What he was about to do, however, carried more danger than anything he had attempted. It was something Martha would have never dreamed of him doing, or capable of doing. He thought a trip to Puerto Rico would give him the best chance of finding the truth about Palmer and Pedro and if Martha had said or done anything that would have given them reason to kill her. He felt that being in San Juan, staying in the same hotel, and having dinner at Pedro's, might lead to some insight as to whether Palmer had any connection with Martha's death.

He would take Jack, Emily, and Britt to Puerto Rico to see what they could find. Emily spoke fluent Spanish after her three-year trip to Central and South America but would not advertise her ability to speak Spanish. She could listen in on any local conversations and help in gathering information from local news and records.

He figured they would just show up and see what happened, which is how he had learned most of his useful information since coming here. In fact, he remembered his first week here when he tried out "Charlie" for the first time. He had followed Jack to the executive airport, watched him take off, then just walked inside and learned that Martha and Britt may have taken a previous flight with Palmer, which was later confirmed by Britt. Now, several months later, in search of information on Martha's trip with Palmer, he had come full circle.

Henry had enlisted Jack to go on this trip, outlining his reason for the whole undertaking—as Jack was unaware of Palmer's and Pedro's recent posting on the suspect list.

"Jack, we're looking into whether Palmer Middleton might have had something to do with Martha's death." It seemed Henry had a new confidant in Jack, so he described how he got to the possibility of Pedro and Palmer killing Martha. Jack couldn't discard the possibility, although he was pretty doubtful that they would do such a thing over what Martha *might* have seen or interpreted.

"If they did do it," Jack told Henry, "you'll need to hire some gunslingers to help out. You might not end up underwater in your car, but there's all kinds of accidents a middle-aged man grieving his wife's death might have. You're a very small fish and could be an irritant to them that they don't need to put up with. You'd be just another unsolved accident."

Henry knew Jack was right, but he had already made up his mind to go and *how* he wanted to get there. A few months before, standing outside the chain-link fence beside the runway, he watched as Palmer's private jet took off. The sight and sound of that takeoff had sent shockwaves through him, which he hadn't felt since riding in his buddy's muscle car back in high school when it burned rubber down Main Street at midnight. Henry was ready to do what was necessary to be sitting in a small jet for takeoff.

He asked Jack, with his connections at Charleston International Airport, to check if there was any way they could catch a ride in a small jet to San Juan. He would not be using the executive airport with one of Palmer's men on the premises. Jack had friends in the jet charter business, and as luck would have it, they were taking a small jet to San Juan the following week for a couple of days. The trip was for a potential buyer of the jet and would be happy to accommodate Jack and have the small group ride along for the cost of a commercial flight for each passenger to help cover expenses. Henry agreed, covering everyone's expenses.

They would pose as friends and family on a trip to reminisce about Martha in a place she had fallen in love with. It would be Henry's first trip out of North or South Carolina, and he looked forward to it with an excitement he hadn't felt in recent memory. Jack and Britt had been there, of course. For Emily, it was her first trip to the island.

Henry slept little the night before takeoff, anticipating actually sitting in the jet. It didn't matter where it was going, other than it was going to take off. He sat beside a window facing Emily, with Jack and Britt across the aisle facing each other. Jack had briefed him the night before that the jet needed about 4,000 feet of runway for takeoff and would climb at about 4,000 feet per minute up to around 40,000-foot altitude and cruise close to 500 mph for their three-hour ride to San Juan. Henry had almost swooned just hearing this; he was already in the clouds.

———

The next morning, the Lear 60 jet stopped at the end of the runway for a moment, spooling up the jets like a Formula One race car on the starting grid. Henry gripped the seats, a wide grin on his face, alternating between looking out the window and laying his head back in the seat with his eyes closed. He looked over at Emily and nodded, as if saying, "Here we go!" The pilot released the brakes, the roar from the jets flooded his head, and the acceleration pushed Henry back into his seat. As he watched the runway lights speed by faster and faster, his heart raced. Before he knew it, the nose pulled up and they shot into the sky. Henry felt his stomach on the verge of erupting. Slowly, he became accustomed to the feeling, laid back, and enjoyed the sensation.

After about ten minutes, the plane leveled off, as did Henry's heartbeat.

"My God, that was everything I thought it would be," he said to no one in particular. He looked over at Emily, who was smiling at him, then over at Jack, who appeared to be sleeping. He gave a thumbs up to Britt.

"Not bad, huh?" said Britt.

Britt walked to the small kitchen and found the coffee maker and fresh muffins. After she had served everyone, she looked at Emily. "I've learned some interesting facts about this island that we're flying to. When Martha and I were in San Juan, we were sitting around the hotel bar one afternoon, and she got into talking about her father who was the DA of Charleston in the midst of the 'white-collar' drug smuggling times along the South Carolina coast, how exciting those stories had been, and that now Puerto Rico was considered the latest hot-spot port of entry for smuggling drugs. I was curious if you have ever thought of going into that side of the law? To me, it would seem more exciting than something like tax law."

"It's strange you should ask, as I've been considering taking some courses in that field. It's specialized with an international flavor."

"Britt," said Henry, "was Palmer part of this conversation when Martha was talking of her experience working with her father and the drug smuggling?"

"I believe so, but we had this same conversation with Pedro and Palmer at dinner at his restaurant, where the man said 'fucking drogas,' as he was escorted out the door. Neither Pedro nor Palmer made any comment and moved the conversation on."

"Britt, do you remember any other comments by Martha," asked Henry, "that might have triggered a reaction from them?"

Britt thought a moment. "I do because it was all so interesting to me when Martha told us that when you fly between Puerto Rico and the US mainland in a private plane, there are no baggage checks or customs of any kind. It's like flying between Charleston and Charlotte in your buddy's plane. You can carry drugs, money, guns, or whatever you want between the two."

"That's right," said Emily. "Most of us think of Puerto Rico almost as another country, not a territory of the US."

"But back to Palmer," said Britt, "I was about to ask him if his firm ever worked in this field of law, thinking he might have some interesting stories to tell, but he shifted the conversation and began talking of where we might go for dinner that night."

A frown on his face, Jack asked Britt, "Are you trying to tie Palmer and Pedro to Martha's death because she outlined how easy it is to move money or drugs between PR and the US…all in front of Palmer? What would make Martha think they were up to something like that?"

"I think she was just making interesting conversation," said Britt. "Nothing had been said or implied that Pedro or Palmer could be doing the same thing."

"And if they are," said Jack, "I think they sure as hell would need more evidence than some bar talk from Martha for reason to kill her."

Henry had a thought and changed the direction of the conversation. "Jack, are you paid by Palmer with a company check?"

"No, I'm paid cash."

"Isn't that a strange way to conduct business?"

"Maybe so, but it's better than a check and I needed the job at the time. I still do."

"Britt tells me Palmer's wife, Rita, has always paid for almost everything in cash," said Henry. "That's odd in this day and age."

"They own the shrimp bar down in Folly Beach," said Britt. "I read somewhere that restaurants are good places to launder money as a lot of cash runs through them."

"Some people still pay in cash?" asked Henry. "I walk around with about three dollars in my pocket. That wouldn't buy me a hot dog."

Emily said, "I think we're reaching here for a motive. There's got to be something more substantial that Martha saw and commented on that alerted them. But Rita's quirky habit of paying cash has been around so long it's almost part of local folklore."

"Martha told me later," said Britt, "that she had become interested in the possibility that Palmer, Pedro, and Rita were all part of a small-time drug operation, an under-the-radar mom-and-pop operation. The thought of it had intrigued Martha, remembering stories her father had told her of tracking down drug smugglers back in the day. 'Just musing,' she had said, 'nothing that concerns me even if it were true.'"

Jack looked at Britt and abruptly changed the subject. "Maybe it was not such a good idea for you to play matchmaker on that trip?"

"What? What are you talking about?" asked Britt.

"Palmer said that since he would not be eating at his father-in-law's house, he'd take us all out to dinner both nights. But *you* suggested he might take Martha out as she was new to the city."

"It sounded to me like a reasonable idea," said Britt. "At the time, I didn't know they would be going to Pedro's restaurant and a man would stumble in talking about drugs."

"It just seemed like you were pushing Martha on Palmer."

"I thought I was doing a favor for Martha. Palmer knows the city as well as he does Charleston and can add interest to any outing."

"Well, he added plenty of interest with dinner at Pedro's," said Jack.

The pilot asked them to prepare for landing, and the discussion came to a halt.

Henry frowned. Something that had just been said sounded off, but he couldn't put his finger on it just then.

# CHAPTER 29

Henry had looked forward to landing in the jet but found the approach and landing nerve-racking. The pilot had to contend with a stiff crosswind, so the plane was pushed around violently before finally touching down on the runway. There was applause for the pilot from those in the cabin. For Henry, he found it quite the opposite of the exhilarating takeoff, and hopefully not a precursor of coming events in San Juan. San Martin Airport sat on the northeast coast of the island, three miles from their hotel in downtown old San Juan. They would be staying in one of Pedro's hotels, the Castile Royal, where Martha and the others stayed on their trip. They called ahead for an SUV to meet them plane-side where they loaded their bags and headed for town.

It was midafternoon when they arrived to check in at the Castile Royal, located down a narrow cobblestone street with tan stucco walls and arched windows and doors. Wrought iron balconies, covered in bright flowers, perched off second-floor bedrooms. They entered through an intricately carved front door where a man behind a polished wood counter met them with a gleaming smile. "Ah, Mr. Jack Townsend. It is good to see you again. And it's Miss Pederson, if I remember correctly? I believe you visited us some months ago. Welcome back." He looked at Emily and Henry, a quizzical look on his face.

Jack helped him out. "This is Emily, the daughter of Martha Willis, who stayed here some months ago. Unfortunately, she died recently in a car accident." Putting his hand on Henry's shoulder, he said, "And this is Henry Willis, Emily's father. They both heard so much about your beautiful city from Martha that they had to come see it and experience it for themselves."

"I understand completely. My name is Manuel, and I welcome you to our beautiful city." He made a slight bow.

Henry noticed he kept glancing at Emily, as if he were unnerved by her. Is it because she was a young and beautiful woman, or because she looked like a reincarnated, throwback Martha? He knew Pedro would know in minutes who had just arrived at his hotel.

After checking into their rooms, they met outside in the courtyard. They took a table near a corner, shaded by palm trees and surrounded by large, pink bougainvilleas. Intricately patterned tiles decorated the shaded seating area. For a few minutes, they sat in silence, taking in the aroma of the flowers and exotic scents of the city. Henry felt like he was on vacation in a different world and momentarily lost sight of the business he'd come to do.

A waiter appeared, a broad smile on his face.

"Hello Mr. Jack and Miss Britt, what a surprise. I normally know when you will be arriving. I see you have brought new friends with you." He looked at Henry and Emily. "Good afternoon, my name is Fernando, but you can call me Freddy."

Henry reached over and shook his hand.

"My name's Henry, Henry Willis, and this is my daughter, Emily. We've never visited Puerto Rico and your beautiful city. Jack and Britt were nice enough to offer to be our guides for a few days."

"Mr. Willis, may I offer my condolences for the loss of your wife. I met her a few times. She was here with Mr. Jack and Mr. Middleton, and of course, Miss Britt. Miss Martha was always a most gracious lady." He looked at Emily. "And Miss Emily, you are as beautiful as your mother."

Henry flinched at the mention of Martha's numerous trips here along with Britt, who had told him she and Martha had only been here once. He'd only been here an hour and Martha's exploits away from home kept expanding. He realized she assumed a complete secondary personality when she came to Charleston.

Henry's conundrum was interrupted by Freddy, who looked at Jack. "May I ask if Mr. Middleton will be joining you as usual?"

"Not this time, Freddy. We're on our own just seeing the sights…a mini vacation for all of us."

"I thought it a little strange to see you in the middle of the week without Mr. Middleton, as you're always here on a weekend. I see now. A mini vacation. Anyway, it's good to have you here no matter what day it is." He smiled. "Well, enough talk, you must be thirsty. What can I bring you?"

Henry squirmed in his seat. He figured Pedro would soon know they were in town and probably not for just sightseeing as they were claiming. He imagined that they would now be under constant surveillance. The short feeling of tranquility he had enjoyed a few minutes before immediately evaporated.

They all ordered drinks, settled back, and refrained from discussing anything about their real reason for being there. Jack and Britt had a few recommendations of restaurants they might go to for dinner. Henry suggested that Jack and Britt each pick their favorite, and that Jack take Emily to his and Britt take him to hers. He added that the gentlemen, of course, would pick up the tabs. Everyone thought this a grand idea. Jack and Britt went in the hotel to make reservations at their favorite restaurants.

Emily reached over and took Henry's hand.

"Dad, I think it was a great idea for you to suggest this arrangement for dinner, especially since we've been all cooped up together for almost four hours on the plane." She smiled at him. "And I think you had it in the back of your mind that you'd like to have a special dinner with Britt in this island atmosphere…especially after all the time you've spent working together. And, of course, I'm excited to have Jack take me to his favorite spot, although I'm not sure what type of place that might be." She laughed. "But I know we'll have fun."

———

In the early evening, the two couples headed off in different directions. Britt and Henry walked a couple blocks until they came to a small restaurant tucked a short distance down a side street. There were only a few other couples eating, as it was still early for most locals to be dining out. They were led to a small, cozy table in the back with a white tablecloth and candle. Henry ordered a bottle of red Spanish wine and a small plate of appetizers. This is perfect, he thought. He wanted to give Britt special thanks for helping him all these months and for being there to prop him up when he was down and encouraging him every step of the way. And even though Martha took care of him all those years, he had discovered that she was not who he thought she was; she had deceived him and cheated on him for years. Henry felt proud of what he had accomplished since beginning his quest for the truth. Who would believe he would be sitting in a restaurant in San Juan, Puerto Rico, quite a different man, in his mind, than had shown up in Charleston some months ago?

It seemed a special night out for them to be in a strange city on an island away from the everyday sights and sounds of Charleston. Britt was dressed in a sleek white dress, blond hair tied at the nape of her neck, her blue eyes sparkling. Flushed by the sight of her, Henry felt like a boy on his first date at the prom.

He put his hand on hers.

"I must admit that I look at you now, not only as a confidant, but as someone I am attracted to. Someone I have affection for." He shook his head at his use of these words. "Please excuse my stilted language. It's been a long time since I tried to express these types of feelings." But he had to tell her. He felt his heart against his chest, and he took a deep breath. He looked up. "I think I may be falling in love with you," he said, taking a healthy drink of his wine. He shook his head, his eyes closed, embarrassed that he'd spoken out like this. It was not in his nature, and he had never said this to anyone other than his wife so long ago.

"I'm just trying to be a comfort for you as you go through this," said Britt. "I'm no therapist, but I don't think this is an unusual reaction under the circumstances." She leaned over and kissed him on the cheek.

Startled for a moment, Henry sat up straight, his eyes wide, heart thumping, not knowing what to say.

"That's very kind of you, Henry. I see you in a new light, as well. You've taken it upon yourself to change from a person that others had molded you to be and have discovered the person you really are. I admire you." She smiled, took his hand, and squeezed it. "Just think, if you can get Martha's death resolved, you can begin a new life."

"I'd like that," he said. "You know, we've become a pretty good team these past months, haven't we?"

"We have, and I've found it a relief from theater work every day. It's actually been kind of exciting. It reminds me of a line in that old Bob Seger song, 'Night Moves,' about 'working on mysteries without any clues,' although the context of the line in that song had quite a different meaning."

"I remember that line when I was in high school *because* of its context."

Britt chuckled, shaking her head. "Working on mysteries without any clues reminds me of that night in the hotel in Mexico when we were on spring break in college. My God, that was almost thirty years ago, but I remember it like it was last week." She stopped, as if debating in her mind whether to continue. She took a drink of her wine and looked at Henry.

"I have never forgotten that night," he croaked, taking a drink.

"This is how *I* remember it," she said, a smile crossing her face. "You and me and Martha had been out drinking all afternoon, and it was almost dark when we made our way back to the hotel. We then smoked some pot I'd managed to find. You and Martha were rookies with pot, and it didn't take long before we decided to take a swim. We changed and jumped in the pool. You got out and lay down in a lounge chair. Martha and I got out, and I went to the room Martha and I were sharing by the pool, to get something.

I forget now. But anyway, when I came out, I didn't see Martha and then spotted her in the pool, underwater. I dove in, pulled her out and got her breathing in a few seconds. I all but carried her to our room, dried her off, and lay her on our bed. I lay down and talked to her until she woke up a few minutes later. It was around then that you stumbled in, looking for us and laying down. We were still high on pot and booze, and being English lit majors, we laughed, telling Martha she had taken belladonna, like Juliet, and fallen into the pool. Do you remember what happened after that, Henry?"

"Kinda," he stammered. "Enough so, I never forgot that night. The next morning, still half glassy-eyed, I wasn't sure if I had dreamed of what we did. I asked both of you what happened. Martha said she was embarrassed to talk about it. I remember you just smiled, which I took as a confirmation of what I probably thought had happened." His heart rate had jumped at the remembrance of that night; he found himself almost breathless.

"We were young, innocent and exploring." said Britt. "It was our version of 'Night Moves.' And thankfully, for all our sakes, it stayed in Mexico."

Regaining his composure, Henry said, "Although it would be laughed off these days." Still, it raced through his mind: if what happened in Mexico, plus his affair with the leggy Italian along with Martha's five-year affair with Jack and God knows what else we don't know about came out…Jesus, we'd be disgraced in absentia. He shook off the thought and carried on.

"But it's been most enjoyable spending time with you and trying to solve the riddle of Martha. And I think we're getting close. Palmer and Pedro appear to have had the motive and I'd bet they had the means to accomplish it, as well. The only problem is, I don't have the means to prove it."

"You're right. That would be a tough job, even for the pros."

"Maybe she just drove into the water by mistake?" said Henry.

"But could you be satisfied with walking away from it and moving on?"

"That's the thing. I can't do that yet."

"Well, let's just keep plugging away and see if we can come up with anything new. Think how far you've come since walking into town thinking for sure that Jack was the guilty one. If you hang around long enough, you might come across the definitive answer of what happened."

"You promise to stick with me?"

"I wouldn't miss it for the world."

# CHAPTER 30

The next morning, after a late breakfast at the hotel, Henry and Emily decided to go to the city library and search for local information on Pedro. Jack and Britt wanted to hang around the pool and go shopping a little later. Henry and Emily went to the Library National to search the records and newspaper articles for anything under Pedro Rodriguez and drug smuggling. Their Google search on the internet had given some information, but Emily wanted to check the local Spanish newspapers for more in-depth information.

They learned that Pedro had been cleared of selling cocaine. Small quantities were involved, and it appeared the police looked the other way. Besides, the police were more interested in the "big dogs." Rumors were that Pedro paid off the police, that he spreads goodwill, gives to charities, and keeps a low profile. Over the years, he had accumulated two worn-down hotels and a restaurant, renovated them both, and had made them very popular, to both tourists and the locals. He was charismatic and had at one time been encouraged to run for mayor of the city. Although he enjoyed great popularity, he decided against running, saying his businesses took all his time. There was nothing definitive pointing to nefarious activities, but he could not dodge the perception that his restaurant and hotels could not provide the change in lifestyle from a struggling grocery store owner to upper middle-class businessman that he had jumped into thirty-five years before. It was believed that he dealt in small-time smuggling on occasion, not enough to gather the interest of the police—a sort of very low-key mom-and-pop operation that didn't seem to disturb anyone, especially the police, who were more than likely getting compensated for looking the other way. It appeared Pedro had been accused of smuggling but never charged. Accommodations, compensations, and agreements had been made.

———

Early that evening, they all gathered together in the courtyard for drinks. Talk was centered on sightseeing banter during vacations taken or on the short list to take, but no shoptalk of Puerto Rico. Freddy and the other servers were pleasant enough but were not the jovial folks they had been upon their arrival. Jack made reservations for dinner at Pedro's restaurant that night. Freddy and the boys were obviously on alert and never far from the conversations.

———

Pedro's was conveniently located just two blocks from the hotel, within easy walking distance. Its exterior looked like a scaled-down version of his hotel—El Castile's little brother.

Inside, dark wood tables were lit with candles; there were also dimly lit wall paintings and a wood-beamed ceiling that gave the place a cozy, secluded atmosphere. Pedro's catered to more affluent locals than tourists, but Henry, Britt, Jack, and Emily garnered little attention other than brief glances from people who knew they were not regulars. They were steered to a table toward the rear of the seating area as a three-piece band of piano, bass, and guitar played softly to one side. Knowing most of the people in the restaurant spoke excellent English, they kept their voices low.

Just after being seated, they saw a tall man walk in and a noticeable increase in alertness by the maître d' and the servers. He stopped by most of the tables, saying a few words to the diners. When he reached Henry's table, he introduced himself and welcomed them to his restaurant. Dressed in a soft white linen suit, a white shirt, and pale blue tie, he looked the part of a well-to-do island businessman. He looked briefly at all of them, his eyes stopping on Emily a few seconds longer, before moving on to the other tables.

Within three minutes, their server brought a bottle of champagne and four glass flutes and asked if he might pour each a glass. Henry asked who had sent this. The server looked over to a large table, nodding toward Pedro, who was looking in their direction. With a smile on his face, Pedro held his glass up in a toast to everyone, then looked at Emily and toasted her. Everyone but Henry raised their glass in a toast. Pedro lost his smile, tilted his head a little, and stared at Henry. In response, Henry raised his glass and set it down without drinking. The others at the table stared at Henry with a look of alarm on their faces. For a moment, Henry stared at his glass of champagne, then pushed it away from him. No one had spoken, as eyes shifted around the table expressing their amazement and fear at Henry's most obvious rebuff of Pedro Rodriguez's toast—in his own restaurant. Only those at Pedro's table and those beside Henry's noticed what had happened. The band played on with the rest of the restaurant being unaware.

"I've lost my appetite," mumbled Henry. He put his napkin on the table, pulling out his wallet. He placed a hundred-dollar bill on the table, the same size dollar bills he knew Pedro had thrown around in front of Martha on her visit here. "That should cover the four glasses of champagne and bread rolls they brought us. I'm leaving. Would anyone like to join me?" He looked around the table. Everyone put their napkins on the table, stood, and walked out.

They walked silently for half a block when Britt said, "Didn't know you had it in you."

Henry thought of what Martha had told him in the restaurant so long ago about his affair. The same words. Henry felt good but thought he might have wet his pants.

"I'm proud of you, Dad," said Emily as she took his hand and squeezed it.

Jack shook his head and said, "Jesus Christ, Henry, you want to get us killed?"

"I didn't like the way he looked at Emily. I think the son of a bitch probably had Martha killed. And there he was, eyeing her daughter, my daughter, in front of all of us. Maybe he can pull that shit here in his city, but not in front of this family."

They stopped at a small restaurant and enjoyed a quiet dinner, along with one too many bottles of wine.

Back at their hotel, they made a point of not going to the bar and decided to meet in Henry's room for a nightcap. Henry opened his door and found an unmarked envelope that had been slid under his door. He opened it and read, *You best not try to fuck with ol' Pedro.*

It was wheels up at sunrise.

# CHAPTER 31

To Henry, the trip to Puerto Rico had seemed like a dream, an adventure to an exotic island with a woman he felt he was falling in love with. And there was Jack, who said he didn't kill his wife, and there was his daughter, who was falling in love with Jack. Henry needed to learn if Palmer and Pedro, and their possible drug smuggling, were connected somehow with Martha's death. It had affected him in a way he couldn't put his finger on. The things he saw, things he heard, things he said. A confluence of thoughts and feelings swirled about, unnerving him. It was all so alien to anything he had ever done or observed. He was unsure it had even happened.

It began with the rush of takeoff in the small jet that sent his heart flying. Then, while airborne, Britt told of Martha's talking in front of Palmer about her knowledge of drug smuggling, little knowing that later Palmer might be implicated in her death. His dinner with Britt, "working on mysteries without any clues," and her bringing up that long ago night in Mexico. She was in the mood to talk sex and drugs. Was it being on an island in the Caribbean that loosens one's tongue? Then he remembered dinner at Pedro's and the note slid under his door, *You best not fuck with ol' Pedro*, and any thoughts of sex and drugs disappeared.

But what doesn't feel right about all this? I need to talk to Emily, my anchor.

———

Henry called her and went over to her house. Emily set out a couple beers and a bowl of mixed nuts. He sat at the end of her couch, with Emily on the armchair beside it. Henry spread out to her where he was with his thinking and how it didn't seem to come together in any orderly fashion.

"Emily, some things said on our trip to Puerto Rico don't seem to add up or make sense to me after thinking back on them. On the flight over there, Jack all but accused Britt of trying to play matchmaker between Martha and Palmer by suggesting that Palmer take Martha out to dinner both nights they were there and show her around. And what struck me…when Britt told me about that trip, she said she couldn't join them for dinner because she had the flu both nights they were there. What does this mean, if anything?"

"Dad, I'm not sure we can come to any conclusion on that," she said. "But you pissed off Pedro, and he retaliated with his copy of your comment to Janice. When she was trying to get information out of you for Palmer, you said, 'You best not fuck with ol' Charlie,' which shows all the Puerto Rico players are in the loop. But none of it gives any credence that they had anything to do with Mom's death. I think they're in the drug business, or something along that line, but that doesn't lead them to sending Mom down a ramp on a rainy night in Charleston. That's a long shot, I believe."

"Who knows what Mom might have said to Palmer," said Henry. "Out on the town two nights for dinner, being wined and dined by the fancy Charleston lawyer on the make. She'd already spouted her knowledge of drug smuggling."

Frowning, he changed direction. "Maybe I'm grasping for straws. Her death was almost too complicated to have been a murder. Too many things had to have fallen in line. Maybe it *was* an accident." Exhaling, he shook his head. "Which is the last thing I want to believe. I don't want to have to look in the mirror to find who was responsible for her death."

"Don't talk like that, Dad," said Emily. "Let's see, maybe we should go back to the beginning and take another look. To the farewell dinner where it all started and…" She reached over and took Henry's hand. "The catalyst for all that happened was the rumor, and you've never said anything about the affair. I've assumed the rumor was true, although no one has ever mentioned a name or any details." She glanced over at Henry.

He nodded slowly, meeting her eyes.

"Emily, the rumor was true. I've never said anything about it to you, or anyone except your mother, because it was embarrassing both for myself and your mother, and her mysterious death superseded everyone's thoughts. The affair was lost in the conversation. It was not even an affair, but a half hour seduction, to my complete surprise, by one of my graduate students, Sophia Bandini, in my office one evening. Why? I don't know. It made no sense to me. I revealed this to your mother that night at dinner in the restaurant." He stopped, looked off, and with tears welling, barely managed to say, "I believe she forgave me."

Emily sat beside him on the couch and hugged him. "Thank you for telling me, Dad, I know how hard it was to retell something like this from your last dinner with Mom."

"Thanks, Emily, your words mean a lot to me." He wiped his eyes and took a deep breath. "Now back to the rumor at the retirement party. Everyone at the college saw us leave early, and anyone present could have been at the garage in less than an hour later. But if there'd been no rumor of the affair, we'd have left the college *after* the retirement dinner and…*I* would have walked with Martha to the garage, since it was three blocks from the college, and we would have passed Chez Toulouse along the way. But it was more likely Martha would have *insisted* on getting the car if we were at Chez Toulouse since the garage was only half a block away. The rumor increased the odds we would leave early and go to Chez Toulouse." Henry looked off a moment. "I've wondered who started the rumor, and why did they do it at the party? To embarrass me in front of everybody?"

"Why would anyone want to do that to you?" said Emily. "You and

Martha were the honorary guests. Maybe someone had heard about it and without thinking, innocently told someone else and it just spread around. *Or,* what if they *knew* how Martha would react and would probably snatch you out of there, and where you'd probably go for dinner. I'm sure there are people who knew Martha well enough and could guess where you would probably go to eat…and possibly think Martha would be the one to go alone to get the car." She thought for a moment. "You know, Britt's been with you through everything since you've been here. What does she think happened?"

"She believes it was an accident. That Martha, after dealing with Jack at the restaurant, having a few glasses of wine with little to eat, lost her focus in the storm and just drove down the ramp by mistake. Which is about where I am right now." He glanced at Emily, finding her staring at him.

"You like her, don't you, Dad?" She smiled.

Caught off guard by the sudden personal question, Henry managed to mutter, "I…must admit I've come to enjoy her company." He hoped he wouldn't have to explain further.

"Hey, it's okay. She's an attractive woman, and you've been working close to her for months. I would expect a connection would be made. And good for you."

Relieved, he said, "Thanks for understanding."

# CHAPTER 32

If Martha was murdered with no evidence of foul play, Henry thought, the killer had to have known some of Martha's proclivities and be physically able to exit through an open car window with water rushing in and swim to shore in the river current and be very lucky. Jack fit the bill on these plus had motive. To a lesser extent, Byron might have managed this, had the motive, but was gutless and probably thought himself too "pretty" to get himself muddied up like this. Palmer and Pedro had the means and possibly the motive to do this between them, but questionable they would have gone about disposing of Martha in such a manner.

Hell, there were a lot of people who could have pulled this off, or someone could have been hired to pull this off. But what could have been their motive? Did Martha have an enemy, or enemies, no one knew about who did it for reasons no one will ever know? This conjecture could go on forever.

Henry had a lot riding on his finding the killer by closing the deal and not hesitating, as he was prone to do. A thought suddenly came to mind, and he called Carl Muncie at the toxicology department, leaving a message asking him if any type of prescribed barbiturate drugs were found in Martha's autopsy.

———

Henry needed to talk to Britt and clear up some of the questions he had. He stopped by her place in the early evening.

"Britt, I don't understand why Martha would go out with Palmer if there was any inkling he was somehow connected with drug dealing or money laundering. He would know who she was and her father's background in drugs in South Carolina in the early '80s. She would be looked at as a possible infiltrator into the operation. And I would have thought you or Jack might have warned her about keeping a tight lip around Palmer, not that she would have heeded your warning."

"Over the years," said Britt, "I found that Martha liked to be on the edge, sometimes. She was on a private jet to an exotic setting in Puerto Rico with a big-time Charleston lawyer, whose wife was absent, and who was more than willing to show her the town. And if Palmer was somehow connected to drug dealings with his father-in-law, who lived in San Juan, what could be more exciting than getting that close to it? It could be a 'made for TV' experience that she could talk about forever. And as you know, no one's going to change her mind once she's locked in on something."

He got up and walked around.

"She became a different person down here. Quite the opposite of the serious professor emerita of Southern College. It was like she was on spring break from college, making up for the conservative, take-no-chances person she presented herself to be when she was a college student and teaching at Southern." He shook his head. "Jesus, it's so hard to comprehend." He slumped down on the sofa, bent over, and rubbed his eyes. "I don't know what to think anymore. We're running out of suspects and even Palmer and Pedro might be a stretch."

"I've thought from the beginning that she drove down the ramp by mistake," said Britt, "and by the time she realized what was happening, she couldn't get herself out of the car. I don't think Jack, Byron, Palmer, or Pedro could, or would, have done it."

"Maybe you're right. Maybe Martha made her first big mistake and it cost her life?" Henry felt defeated, and it made him mad. His jaw tightened as he turned his head to look out the window. "My gut tells me, though, it wasn't an accident." He sat up straight. "I bet there's somethin' I ain't seein'."

She rested her head on his shoulder. "You might be right, Charlie," she said, chuckling.

"I'll just try lookin' harder," he said.

"I think you need to take a break from working on these mysteries. It might give you a new perspective."

"I'm thinkin' you're right. Seems my head's been wrapped up pretty tight recently." He leaned back on the sofa and closed his eyes. Henry enjoyed being Charlie. Charlie could say and do things that Henry couldn't or wouldn't. And he had recently found that Henry had almost become Charlie. He switched gears. "Could I take another look at those receipts you had from Martha's affair with Jack? I've calmed down enough now to look at them a little closer."

She brought out the boxes. Henry began carefully going through them, putting the receipts in stacks with the same date. He found that every three or four months, there would be a grouping of receipts, sometimes for one day, others over a two- or three-day period. Most were for restaurants outside of what's considered downtown Charleston, with some in Mt. Pleasant and the surrounding islands. There were receipts also for purchases from some of the finer men's stores. What he *didn't* find were any receipts from hotels. This struck him a little strange if she were having an affair and basically footing the bill. Although Jack did have a condo which would explain no receipts. Or maybe Jack was telling the truth when he told me it had been a platonic relationship?

"Did Martha ever give you any indication she ever slept with Jack?"

Britt scrunched her face for a moment. "You know, I don't think she did, but she never said much of anything about her relationship with Jack. She always stayed in a hotel when she was down here and put that on her regular card. She could come into town and I might never see her, or know she had been here, until I saw the statements and she gave me receipts. And she used a second phone when she was down here seeing Jack."

All Henry got out of this exercise was that the receipts didn't confirm they had slept together, which provided a certain amount of relief to him.

"Martha had an affair on and off for five years and kept it a secret," he said. "I had one for one half an hour and the whole world knew about it. How is that possible? And Martha found out at the retirement dinner of all places. Jesus, was she mad! Come to think of it, Britt, do you know who started the rumor? And why do it at our going away party? Was someone trying to embarrass me for some reason in front of Martha and everyone? Not to mention the embarrassment to Martha. I'm lucky to have survived dinner that night." Out of breath, he looked at her, his eyes wide, his arms raised questioningly.

"Henry, I…" She stopped, thinking for a moment. "All I remember is how shocked I was to hear of it."

Henry couldn't let it go, his temper rising at the thought of it again. "*Who* would do such a thing, and *why* would they do it?"

Britt shook her head. "I don't know. It doesn't make any sense to me."

"Jesus, I'm so tired of all this," said Henry. "I need to go back to the apartment, take a drink, and lie down." He rose to his feet, looked down at Britt, and smiled. "Thanks for listening to me rant."

Henry returned to his apartment, poured a small glass of cognac, and sat in his easy chair. He looked out the window, watching as the sky turned pink with the setting sun. He sat there in a daze as he sipped his drink thinking he was missing something. Then it came to him.

"The rumor was *not* the beginning of everything," he said aloud, "it was the so-called *affair*!" Jesus, it was right in front him. He rubbed his eyes. His head hurt, and he walked into the bedroom and fell on his bed facedown. His mind flooded with remembrances of that seminal evening in his life at the college that changed everything:

*It was early evening, the last week in the semester, with little or no traffic in the halls of Southern College. Henry sat at his small conference table, antici-pating the arrival of the intriguing, young Italian grad student, Sofia Bandini. It began as an innocent request from Sofia the week before for extra help with the somewhat obscure secondary interpretation of Romeo and Juliet. She was already a B+ student in his class, and Henry was inspired by her diligence in wanting to learn more about a subject than his course required. It was now her third after-hours visit to his office, and this evening would complete her extra study with him. Henry had to admit that he had come to look forward to his sessions with her. Henry admired beauty and intellect and had become almost mesmerized by Sophia's presence and would sometimes find himself in a daze during his after-hours sessions with her.*

*As he sat waiting for her arrival, the dream he had of Sophia the night before replayed in his mind yet again, and it still startled him. He was running with her down a grass hill toward the lake, holding hands and laughing together. He was to take her sailing in his small boat. They reached the dock, but the sailboat was not there. He was at a loss for what to do. She smiled and said, "We'll find something else to do," and pulled him down to lie beside her on the soft grass. She leaned over on top of him and began kissing him, unbuckling his belt when he suddenly woke up, his heart beating. He looked over to see Martha sleeping soundly beside him and he held his breath, fearing somehow his wife knew what he had been dreaming.*

*Still in the dream, Henry was startled when there was a soft knock on the door, and he heard the door open. When he looked up and saw her, tall and slim, her dark hair falling over her shoulders, dressed in a short black skirt and a white silk blouse, it took his breath away. He cleared his throat.*

*"Good evening, Sophia," and felt it best if he stayed seated. He motioned to the chair beside him. "Let's sit over here at the conference table. I have a book to show you that may help clarify the last few points we need to cover."*

*"Thank you again, Professor Willis, for taking the time with me," she said, coming to the table, leaning over, and placing a small white box on the table in front of him. Henry couldn't help but glance at the swell of her breasts when she*

*leaned over. Smiling, she said, "A small gift for you and me to share, if you don't mind." The hint of a delicate perfume enveloped him as she sat down beside him. He was speechless but managed to take the top off the box, which revealed two dark chocolates.*

*"There's one for you and one for me," she purred. "Go ahead and try one."*

*He nodded, and with a shaking hand, he was just able to pick up a chocolate and get it into his mouth. Her pale blue eyes never left his as she picked up her chocolate, opened her lips, and slid it in. Slowly chewing, she slipped her hand under the table to his knee, slid it up his leg, and waited. Henry jumped a bit at this and stopped breathing for a moment, his eyes wide. Aroused, he began breathing heavily as he looked into her eyes. His lips parted, and he became a little dizzy.*

*"I like your chocolates. Thank you," he whispered. "I…I don't know what to say."*

*"Shh…shh…" she said softly." Her hand moved up his leg, and he almost swooned when she found what she was looking for. She leaned toward him and, with her other hand, unbuttoned two more buttons of her blouse. Henry could see she was not wearing a bra. He blinked, his mouth open. She reached over and took his hand, placing it on one of her exposed breasts. Smiling, she covered his hand with hers and pressed it against her. She was holding him beneath the table and began to move her hand ever so slowly, rubbing him until his body stiffened and his head fell back, his eyes closed. He sighed, his hand tightening on her breast and then releasing and dropping to the table. "My God," he croaked.*

*She smiled and slowly got up, leaned over, and whispered in his ear, "Good night, Professor, and thank you for all your help." Straightening up, she let herself out.*

# CHAPTER 33

The seduction was the beginning of everything. And Henry had a nagging feeling that Sophia Bandini had somehow played a role in the intricate story leading to Martha's death. But something was missing. Her seduction of him appeared to be the inciting incident, but how did she connect with him? Was it a seduction of her own choice, and then by chance, uncovered and whispered throughout the retirement party? Henry had been curious, over the months since the retirement party, that not one person had called or mentioned the name of the grad student who he allegedly had the affair with. Understanding the reticence of most people to bring it up with him, surely George, his best friend and confidant, would have mentioned Sophia Bandini to him. Strange.

He called George.

"George, it's me, Henry. Hope everything is good with you. Bet your getting pumped up for fall semester. I just had a quick question for you."

"Good to hear from you, and yes, everything is good and fall semester is bearing down on us. How can I help?"

"A curious question. Do you know who I had the so-called affair with?"

"No, I don't, and I've never heard anyone say who they thought it was, or guessed it was, but most couldn't believe you'd do such a thing. I didn't ask you, figuring if you wanted me to know you would have told me."

"That's true and thanks for your consideration. That's strange, don't you think, George, the silence of her name from all sides? What's juicier than an over-the-hill professor having an affair with a young grad student? Seems like the gossip queens would have spread her name around by sundown the following day."

"It sure is strange. Actually, it would have been on Facebook before dinner that night."

"Well, George, you will be the first one to know, but don't tell a soul. It was Sophia Bandini."

"What? You're kidding me, aren't you, Henry?"

"So, you know who she is?"

"She came in to try out for a part in this coming semester's production. She walked in, and everything came to a stop. I couldn't get anyone to pay attention. And I have to include myself on that list. Jesus, Henry, how did that happen?"

"It wasn't really an affair. It was more like a short seduction in my office. And to answer your question, *I* didn't make it happen. And that's why I'm calling. I don't know why she picked me out to seduce, and I thought maybe you could help get some background on her. Maybe from her application to the college."

"I'll get right back to you…Sophia Bandini? Remarkable."

A few days later, George sent a summary of Sophia's resume for admittance to Southern College:

"She attended private schools in New York her entire academic career, including college in upstate New York. In her application for the graduate program at Southern, she wrote, 'I naturally aspire to attain the most knowledge possible in a course of my liking. I would like to come to Southern College in Asheville, North Carolina, for my graduate degree in English literature and to study under Professors Henry and Martha Willis, two of the more renowned scholars of English literature.' By the way, she's presently on campus taking additional courses."

To Henry, this probably answered why she took the extra class in the evening. But it didn't give a clue as to why she had seduced him. He needed to ask her why, realizing any talk with Sophia would be best held in person—considering the delicacy of their last meeting together and how that final class was concluded. He didn't feel a phone call or email would be appropriate. He would drive up to the college and see her. He emailed her, asking if he could speak to her for a moment on a serious personal matter of his. After some hesitation, she agreed and said to come by her house the following Saturday morning.

———

Henry became anxious days ahead of his appointment, just thinking of her and what he would say—not to mention the special events of their last meeting. He practiced what he would say to her, repeating it to himself on his drive up to Asheville. His phone map led him to her address just outside the city, her house set on a quiet, shaded street of small houses, all with neatly trimmed lawns and flower beds.

As he walked to her front door, he remembered the similar feeling of anxiety when he first arrived in Charleston. When approaching Emily's house, he didn't know how he would be received after their recent quarrels. This time, his trepidation was quite different in that, at first she wouldn't recognize him, but he knew how to overcome that. The difficulty was starting a conversation with her almost four months after she had left him speechless sitting at his office table.

He rang the doorbell. She opened the door wearing a pale blue Southern College sweatshirt, designer jeans, and a quizzical look on her face.

"Hi, Sophia, it's Henry Willis. You may remember me as your professor at Southern College last spring term, for your graduate work in English literature."

"I remember Professor Willis, but you're not him."

"You may have heard that my wife, Martha, died mysteriously less than a month after our last session, where you shared a small box of chocolates with me at the table in my office. Where you unbuttoned your blouse and had one of your hands under the table on my leg." He looked at her with a small smile and noticed her eyes down, blushing a bit with a nod of her head. He continued on. "And since the death of my wife, I have worked at upgrading my physical appearance to take on the task of trying to solve her mysterious death."

"Oh, of course, please come in, Professor." She stepped back. "Please have a seat. May I get you something to drink? I have hot coffee, if you would like, or maybe a soft drink?"

"Coffee would be fine. With sugar, please, if you have it." He sat in one of the armchairs that faced out through a giant sliding glass door that revealed a beautiful view of a grass lawn sweeping down to the French Broad River.

She returned with the coffee and took a seat across from him. "You told me on the phone you had a serious personal question to ask me?"

"Yes, I do," he said. "Your grade in my course at the time I last saw you was a B+. Your extra work had brought you to an A, so your special treatment of me that evening, I believe, was not to raise your grade or save you from failing the course. So, I must assume there was another reason. And I say that because your seduction of me, I believe, started a chain of events that culminated in my wife being murdered."

"I…I don't understand how that could be possible."

"Did someone ask you to seduce me? I'm not the type to be targeted for seduction, other than for the enhancement of their grade. Your grade was already above average and not in need of enhancement, so I'm curious about your actions that last evening. Can you tell me why you seduced me?"

Swallowing hard, her face flushed. "My mother asked me to do it."

"And who is your mother?"

"Britt Pedersen."

# CHAPTER 34

Stunned, Henry was speechless. This was the missing piece in the puzzle. His head spinning, he felt he had just received a blow to his chest. *My God,* he thought. He leaned back, unable to absorb what he had just been told.

He took a deep breath and pushed on.

"You have her eyes and her smile," he said, "the only hint that she could be your mother. Did she say why she wanted you to do this?"

"She said it would help her to move toward a very happy life with someone she loved."

"And that was all?"

"Yes, that was it."

"Why was being her daughter never mentioned, or a matter of record, when you applied to Southern?"

"Before I was born, she came down from her home in New York to go to Charleston College, where she met Martha. After graduating, she returned to New York. There she met Antonio Bandini, and after a very short romance, I was born out of wedlock, and she gave me his surname. But he disappeared shortly after I was born.

"My mother told me years later that she was too young to try and raise a child and asked her mother to raise me. I believe she was ashamed of me. As it turned out, I was lucky. Her mother and father were both very loving.

Being well off financially and highly educated, they saw to it that I went to the best schools and college in the area. I saw my mother for short periods when I was young, when she worked at the college in town.

"But when she returned to Charleston years ago, I seldom saw her. Our only communication was a birthday card or Christmas card, and they came only occasionally. She disappeared from my life. I was forced to stand on my own. I *had* to, and I have."

"This is all a little hard to comprehend, Sophia. It's a sad tale to hear of a mother who treated her own daughter like this."

"I am very sorry if my actions with you that evening led to the death of your wife. How could my mother use me to help kill a person? I never realized just how cold-hearted she could be."

"Why did you do this for the mother who abandoned you?"

"I thought it might be a step forward, having a relationship with her."

Henry shook his head. Britt had used the daughter she had abandoned to set in motion her scheme to kill her best friend. Henry was incredulous at the thought of Britt committing the premeditated murder of his wife. Furious for not having at least considered Britt as a possible suspect early on, he was most of all angry at himself for being duped by her.

She had thought it out, planned it out, and used her daughter to initiate her murder scheme. No wonder she never asked me who I had the affair with. He was torn about confronting her, but any feelings he had for her had quickly dried up as he assembled the pieces of the puzzle that led inexorably to her as the killer. Any small particle of hope that he was mistaken had been crushed. My God, he thought, she almost had me believing it was an accident, which would have been the cleanest break for her. There would be no messy trials with accused suspects that could drag on forever. It was as if it *were* an accident, just like the police ruled months ago. We can just get on with our lives and move on. Jesus, and I was so close to agreeing it was an accident. I even told her I was falling in love with her. But he wouldn't hesitate and lose his way again. He would ask Sophia to come to Charleston to witness how he would prove Britt was responsible for Martha's death.

"Will you come back with me to Charleston and face your mother? You need to hear why she had you create the incident that was the start of everything that ended with my wife's death."

"Yes, I will," she said softly, nodding as if in resignation of what was to come.

————

Believing that Britt would have to confess after hearing Henry's proof she was the killer, Henry thought it best to have witnesses who knew her present for her confession. He called Emily first, explained that his "affair" was with the grad student Sophia Bandini, who turned out to be Britt's daughter. He explained that she had been asked by Britt to seduce him and unknowingly produce "the affair" accusation. He was bringing her back to Charleston to confront her mother. He asked Emily to meet him when he arrived back.

He called George and told him what he found out from Sophia and a summary of where things stood with her, asking him if he wouldn't mind meeting him in Charleston. Henry explained to him why nobody knew who he had the affair with. Only three people knew what had happened: himself, Sophia, and Britt, a tight little circle, none of whom had a reason to advertise who was involved in the affair, except Britt. He knew now that Britt had started the rumor at the retirement party. Martha had asked him who had seduced him at dinner that last night and he told her, but she didn't live long enough to share it with anybody—not that she would have.

Henry called Britt, asking if he could stop by that evening and talk for a moment. He promised to fill her in when he got there. Sophia rode with him to Charleston, knowing that George could take her back to Asheville.

————

Unlike his last trip to Charleston, some months before, Henry was filled with the trepidations and uncertainties of what he was getting himself into. It reminded him of how far he had come. Now, he was carrying the final piece of the puzzle to Charleston to prove his wife's best friend was her killer.

He drove ten miles an hour over the speed limit.

# CHAPTER 35

Henry met up with Emily and George in Charleston, and they headed for Britt's condo. Henry knocked on her door, with Sophia standing beside him and George and Emily just behind them.

The door opened. Britt looked at Henry, and when she saw Sophia, her eyes widened, and her mouth dropped open. She barely glanced at Emily and George. Britt closed her eyes as she stepped back for them to enter. She motioned to them to have a seat, without saying a word.

As she sat down across from them, she said in a halting voice, "What brings all of you here, together?"

"I believe you know," said Henry in a flat voice.

"I…I'm not sure what you're talking about," stammered Britt.

"Yes, you do," said Henry. "I find it sad and ironic to learn that you used your daughter, who you abandoned, to be in the first scene of your choreographed tragedy that only you could produce. And she now appears in the last scene to bring an end to the mystery. I admit it was a very clever operation you put together, and everything worked like clockwork. You even managed to have a storm that night to help cover your deed."

"Sometimes you just get lucky," she said, almost defiantly.

"Goddamn you!" yelled Henry as he rose, fists clenched. Shaking, he got himself under control and sat back down. "You are a cold-hearted bitch," he hissed.

Taking a deep breath, he started right in.

"You knew Martha better than anyone and knew how she would react in most situations, didn't you? You knew the rumor of 'the affair' that spread at the retirement party would embarrass Martha, and she would drag me out of the party and go to Chez Toulouse, our favorite restaurant. At the time, we thought how lucky we were to get our usual table by the window. Francois later told me you called, weeks before, and asked him to have our window seat available around 6:00 p.m. that day, and by God, you got us there right on time, didn't you?" He stared at her for a moment, waiting for a reaction. None came. She sat rigid in her chair, her face showing no emotion.

"Then came the tricky part—getting Jack Townsend to show up, unannounced, when we were there. I asked Jack how he came to be at the restaurant, all dressed up in a coat and tie, when we were there—at the beginning of a severe thunderstorm, no less. He said you told him we would probably be there around 6:00 p.m., so he could just drop by for a chat. You even knew Martha would probably say something that would provoke Jack, and he would storm out, raging at her, and become the prime suspect, in case you needed one. It all worked perfectly, didn't it?"

Detecting a slight smile on her face, he stood and pointed a finger at her.

"Wipe that fucking smile off your face!"

Once her smile faded, he sat down and continued.

"You also knew Martha would *insist* on getting the car, no matter what the weather, and would deliver herself to you in the garage—alone. You waited near our car and for Jack to disappear. You walked up soaking wet, saying your car wouldn't start and could she give you a ride home. 'Of course, anything for my best friend,' she probably said. Her last words to you. You even produced a small of cup of wine to share in the horrible weather. In the cup, you had a splash of your belladonna, found present in her blood from the autopsy, to keep her drowsy long enough for you to switch seats with her. And you ripped off the chain around her neck that held her glasses. Was it so she would have trouble recognizing who was killing her, if she came to, and you would have to look her in the eyes? I happened to spot the glasses and chain when you sent me to your bathroom one evening to get some Advil. At the time, I was afraid to question you and appear to be accusing you.

"Another stroke of luck for you was that the garage power was off in the storm, along with the cameras, so you didn't have to use your disguise, which I saw in your closet—to drive out of the garage. Again, I was afraid to question you, as I thought I might be accusing you. All of this came into context when I learned you used Sophia to start everything.

"So, you drove to the ramp, switched her back into the driver's seat, buckled her up, leaned over, and drove her into the river. Leaving the front seat windows down, you went through the open passenger window and swam to shore. The flowing tide being no trouble for you, the ex-lifeguard who had, ironically, rescued Martha from drowning in a riptide at the beach, back in a more friendly time. Oh, and you removed her dog Fluffy's front seat restraint, so it wouldn't tangle up Martha switching her around on the bench seat. You even tossed her purse that she always kept beside her left leg over to the passenger side floor, so you wouldn't get tangled up. You came ashore in the rainstorm, walked back to your car in the garage, and went home—returning Emily's call to you from the garage that night. You had been busy with Martha at the boat ramp when we called. So, you got cleaned up and joined us in the search for Martha even though you knew exactly where she was. You played it perfectly. Did I miss anything?"

Britt stared, still silent.

"And you used your abandoned daughter, Sophia, to unknowingly be the lead character in act 1 of the tragedy that ended with you murdering Martha. And Sophia told me she did it hoping to begin a relationship with you. You—are—evil!"

There was silence.

"You were Martha's best friend," said Henry. "Why would you want to kill her?"

"For you."

"For me?"

"It was the only way I would have a chance of getting you."

"Getting me?"

"I've loved you since college and Mexico."

"So you killed her to be with me?"

"Yes. I thought I was lucky when you decided to come to Charleston and have me work with you. We'd have time to reconnect and thought you would, in the end, decide it was an accident."

"This is hard to believe," said Henry, his head spinning.

"No, it isn't," blurted Sophia. "She abandoned me, her only child, so I wouldn't saddle her with being a single mother when it might hinder her career and embarrass her. That's how cold-blooded she is, and killing her best friend to get her husband was the 'coup de grâce' in her life. And to think she called me to help her initiate her plan for revenge shows how little she cared for me. My one interaction with her in years, and it was to make me an accessory to murder." She stared at her mother, who would not meet her eyes. "May you go to hell for what you've done to me, and to your best friend, and to her husband!"

Britt had not moved during this, but tears now appeared in her eyes.

"I am calling the police now," said Henry. "It would be best if you sat right there until they arrive." He pulled his phone from his pocket and called them.

"Hello, my name is Henry Willis. I have a person with me who just confessed to killing my wife, Martha Willis, about three months ago here in Charleston at the new boat ramp on Third Street. I would appreciate your sending the appropriate officers to the following address and taking her into custody." He gave them Britt's address. "Thank you. We'll wait for you here."

"Please don't do this, Henry," Britt pleaded. "I love you. We can go to Mexico."

"It's too late for Mexico."

"I can make you feel young again."

"I bet you could."

"Well, that settles it then, Charlie."

"But I'm Henry, and I want you to sit right there and not move."

"Yes…okay," she said in a low voice.

They sat in silence for a few minutes. Looking at Sophia, Britt said, "All I ever wanted was the best for you, Sophia. I knew I couldn't be the mother you needed, and my mother was much more suited to raise you."

"Is that your excuse?" asked Sophia. "I almost feel sorry for you, if that's how your mind works. And after twenty-five years, you reach out to me for a favor—of all things. And in good spirit, I did it for you, hoping somehow this might lead to a connection with you again…because you're my *real* mother. And now I must live with the realization that what I did was not the first act of reconciliation between us, but the first act of a murder by you. That's how I'll remember you."

The doorbell rang.

# EPILOGUE

Under clear blue skies, a cool early autumn breeze and the late morning sun lifted Henry's spirits. Smiling, he strolled down the sidewalk toward Chez Toulouse. He had just driven in from Asheville and was looking forward to his luncheon date with Emily and Jack. It had been about a month since Britt Pederson had confessed to the premeditated murder of Martha Willis. She was being held without bail. In that time, Henry had returned to his home in Asheville to gather himself the best he could; this was not easy following his tumultuous months in Charleston—even though the time he spent there had transformed his life and who he had become. He sold his house in Asheville and bought a condo in downtown Charleston to begin his new life.

He had forgiven Martha for her "affair" with Jack and her behavior on trips to Charleston. He understood his head had been buried in the sand emotionally all those years. He had been afraid of stepping out of his cocoon and regaining his balance in life. Martha had protected him all those years, so he could become the esteemed professor he was capable of being. But he understood why Martha had gone on "spring break" from time to time. It was to balance her life, so she would have the mental energy to take care of him. He wished she were waiting for him at the restaurant, and that they would be somewhat equals—not only in the academic arena, but also as husband and wife. On equal footing, emotionally.

He opened the door to the restaurant and was met by a beaming Francois who, with much fanfare, directed him toward their table by the window. But this time, it was Emily facing him. She was smiling, and Jack was sitting beside her. Emily stood as he approached and came around and hugged him.

"Welcome to your new hometown, Dad," she said, kissing him on the cheek.

Jack stood. "Welcome back, Henry," he said, shaking his hand.

Smiling, Henry sat down across the table from Emily and Jack.

"Nice of y'all to invite me to lunch in my favorite restaurant…and by the window, no less."

"And I'm sitting here behaving myself," said Jack, grinning.

Henry nodded. "I bet that good-looking lady next to you has something to do with that."

Emily shook her head. "Well, I'm not sure about that, but we've ordered a 'cheese and meat' platter and a bottle of sauvignon blanc for us to share. How does that sound?"

"Sounds just fine to me," said Henry. "Jack, I have to ask, have you taken up white wine now?"

"Yep, just one of the finer things in life your daughter has introduced me to." He reached over and took her hand.

Henry noticed that Jack suddenly stiffened and sat up straight when he looked toward the front door. Henry turned to see a man and woman being led to their table, passing directly by them. It was the same man who had laughed at Jack in the bar a few months before.

The man stopped at their table and looked at Jack.

"Well, if it isn't the guy who gave me therapy advice in the bar. You waiting for the lady sitting beside you to wipe you off the slate?" He smiled.

Jack began to rise out of his seat but stopped and sat back down. He looked up at the man.

"There's no chance of that." He smiled. "You should try the sauvignon blanc. It's quite good." Nodding at the man, he turned back to Emily. "Now, where were we?"

The man stared at Jack a moment, shook his head, and walked on.

"Well done, Jack," said Emily.

Henry looked at Jack, his mouth half open.

"Emily is the therapist I've been looking for," said Jack, leaning over and putting his arm around her.

"Since we're in a feel-good mood," said Henry, "I have some good news to share with you. Carl Muncie, the toxicologist who performed the autopsy on Martha, and who I got in that bad fight with in high school, has apparently forgiven me to a certain extent. He invited me to have lunch with him and a few of his colleagues next week. I had asked him to do some extra work on Martha's toxicology report that turned out to be a key part of the evidence against Britt at her trial. He received some sort of commendation for going out of his way to help in 'an everyday man's search for the truth,' as the newspaper put it."

"That's great news, Dad. Maybe you can now put that whole incident behind you. And since we're on a roll and staying in the good mood of things," said Emily, "Jack and I would like to take you on a vacation to a Caribbean island where they serve umbrella drinks."

"Does it have white sand and clear water?" asked Henry.

"It sure does."

"Well then, I'm all in."